FIRST
ISLAND
COVER GIRL

FIRST ISLAND COVER GIRL

ANNICE BROWNE

authorHOUSE®

AuthorHouse™
1663 Liberty Drive
Bloomington, IN 47403
www.authorhouse.com
Phone: 1-800-839-8640

© 2012 by Annice Browne. All rights reserved.

No part of this book may be reproduced, stored in a retrieval system, or transmitted by any means without the written permission of the author.

Published by AuthorHouse   11/30/2012

ISBN: 978-1-4772-4642-9 (sc)
ISBN: 978-1-4772-4643-6 (e)

Any people depicted in stock imagery provided by Thinkstock are models, and such images are being used for illustrative purposes only.
Certain stock imagery © Thinkstock.

This book is printed on acid-free paper.

Because of the dynamic nature of the Internet, any web addresses or links contained in this book may have changed since publication and may no longer be valid. The views expressed in this work are solely those of the author and do not necessarily reflect the views of the publisher, and the publisher hereby disclaims any responsibility for them.

Introduction

This story is about two families and four generations: great-grandparents, grandparents, parents, and their children. The journey begins with two school friends Dorothy Cunningham and Wilma Portland during the late forties. Dorothy's parents are Samuel and Mary, and she has two older siblings, Alfred, and Cynthia. Wilma has an older brother Barry, and her parents are Peter and Melinda Portland.

After Dorothy and Wilma got married, they lived in the same village. The two ladies husbands, Malc Melrose and Joshua LeBoun were all good friends from school days. Malc's parents are Claudius and Doreen Melrose. Jack and Wendy LeBoun are Josh's parents.

Later years, Malc and Dorothy Melrose had three children Betsie, Annette, and Adam. Wilma and Joshua LeBoun had four children Sam, James, Gideon and Laverne.

As the long friendship between both families progressed into early seventies third generation children are now grown-ups. Annette Melrose and Gideon LeBoun fell in love, got married, and united the Melrose and LeBoun as one big happy family.

When the story unfolds further, the main character is Mari LeBoun, she is forth generation of this dynasty. Mari is Annette and Gideon's first born daughter. One day when Mari was just twelve years of age, she was sitting with her two grandmothers admiring some supermodels in a fashion magazine. Mari told her grandmothers that she would like a career as a fashion model. But Mari grandmothers didn't like her career choice and they tried to discourage her, even after some of her family had disapproved, Mari was determined to pursue her career. She was driven by her ambition, and it was obvious she was growing up into a confident young lady as a result. Mari was quite an inspiration especially to her Mum, and she had persuaded her to follow her dreams change career from an airport checking desk assistant to become a teacher.

Mari worked diligently to succeed in her career, and in the end she had accomplished her dreams.

Chapter 1

Wedding Plans

Annette Melrose and Gideon LeBoun had planned their wedding date, Saturday, June 20, 1970, at the Bluemount Methodist Church, and Reverend Rory Monsolo will perform the wedding ceremony. The Melrose and LeBoun families had arranged a meeting with Rev. Monsolo to discuss wedding plans on Thursday, September 14, 1969, at three o'clock. But shortly before that time, the heavens opened, and heavy rain, lightning, thunder, and strong hurricane winds raged through the island.

Annette's, Dad Malc was standing by the window, looking out over the huge back garden at his home when he noticed lightning flashed between the tall trees. He saw flames flicker through the branches and then noticed sparks that caused him to jump back instantly.

Malc was startled by what he had seen and he shouted to his wife, "Dot, we can't go out until this storm passes!"

Dorothy said, "Let's ring Josh and Wilma to cancel the meeting with Rev. Monsolo. Okay, Malc? After that, we should ring Rev. Monsolo to reschedule the meeting, because I'm afraid of thunder and lightning."

"Do you remember what happened to Carolina?" Malc said. "During a thunder storm she decided to shelter under a big mango tree from the heavy rain, and when the storm passed one of her friends found her burnt out body. She was struck by lightning and electrocuted. Mind you, they say the chance of being struck by lightning is a rare occurrence, and that was most unfortunate for Carolina. She was just fourteen years old."

♣♣♣♣♣

Josh was standing by the window close to the telephone table in his lounge when Malc's call came through; he picked up the phone immediately.

"Hello?" Malc said.

Josh replied, "Oh hi, Malc! I was just about to ring you. This storm means business; I think we should postpone the meeting with Rev for another day."

Malc said, "Yes, we were thinking the same thing, as storms nowadays could kill people!"

Josh said, "Okay Malc; I'll ring Rev. Monsolo and rearrange the meeting for another day. I will let you know what date we agree on; talk to you soon."

Malc said, "Okay, bye."

Josh dialled the minister straight after he ended his conversation with Malc.

"Hello Rev."

Rev. Monsolo said, "Oh hello Josh!"

"Bad storm; I don't think we should venture out in this. Can we meet another evening?"

Rev. Monsolo said, "Sunday evening after mass looks good for me."

"That should be okay for both families, as we would be at church service. So we will see you then."

Rev. Monsolo said, "All right, stay safe, God bless."

The storm roared nonstop for a further two hours; coconut trees swayed, banana trees fell, and some sheets of galvanised roofing blew off houses. Malc turned the TV on but the picture was a bit blurry so he turned it off and switched on the radio instead. The announcer was warning people to stay indoors, as the strong winds were too dangerous. Then he said, "Hurricane Zudy is a category five storm, and very dangerous. This storm could last an hour or more, please stay indoors and stay calm."

People on the island sat indoors nervously, praying hard that their homes would withstand the vicious storm. Around six o'clock, the wind had ceased but it was still raining. Malc got up from where he was sitting next to Dorothy and walked over to the window.

"I think the worse is over," he said.

Dorothy said nervously, "Is that vicious storm over?"

Malc was still looking out of the window; he said, "Yes, it's just raining now." Without looking back at his wife, he said, "Mr Joseph's roof garn, and the two tall trees that used to block our sight are uprooted; I can see Calliaqua Village now."

Dorothy joined her husband to check the damage for herself; she said, "Thank God we are alive! I'd better call the children."

First, she called Annette, who was over at the house Gideon was building to move into after they were married. Gideon is in the property building trade and he runs a prestigious business.

Annette answered the telephone and said, "Hello Mum; Gideon and I are okay, but some houses over here have damaged roofs, and there are many trees uprooted, especially the banana trees. Also, you know that lovely grafted mango tree in Mrs Beverson's garden, that's garn!"

Dorothy said, "Oh what a pity. Still, that's only minor; glad you kids are okay."

As soon as Dorothy placed the receiver down, a call came in from her eldest daughter Betsie.

"Hello Mum, are you and Dad okay?"

"Yes, how about you; asked Mum?"

Betsie said, "We are safe but the garden shed blew away, and a few banana trees in the back garden are down, but other than that we are fine."

Finally, Dorothy rang her son Adam.

Adam said, "Hi Mum, what a storm; it was wicked! I took plenty of photos on my camera. I will scan them on my PC."

"Son what are you talking 'bout? What PC?" Adam said, "Mum, my computer."

"Oh, that machine."

"Mum, one day I promise I would teach you how to use the Internet and send email messages to families and friends."

"Son; I think that is something for young people!"

"No Mum, 'never say never'; isn't that what you are always telling us? Nothing is too big to conquer; the Internet makes the world a smaller place! I can contact any part of the world from my computer.

"Yes, I will show you the photos later."

"When later; asked Adam's mum?"

"I should be home about ten o'clock, because I'm going to watch a play some friends and I had filmed. We are hoping to make it big at the box offices all over the Caribbean. It will be a two part drama about a teenage girl's reckless life."

"That sounds real and easy to emulate . . . my son!"

Did you speak with Annette and Betsie?"

"Yes son, all are safe."

"Love you, Mum."

"Love you too, son. Bye!"

Malc said; "What are we having for supper? That storm knocked me for six; I feel tired and hungry now."

"We could have the leftover pilau rice and chicken with a bit of salad. Adam is staying out late so he doesn't need supper; we could have it with a big cup of ovaltine, because it's nearly bedtime . . ."

Malc said; "bedtime? It's only half past seven, and there is boxing match on TV at eight o'clock."

"You and your boxing; that game should be banned; two grown men in a ring punching the life out of each other."

"And getting paid good money to do it; Malc remarked! Do you know how many boxers become millionaires?"

"Yes, look at Muhammad Ali; after all those blows he took to his head and, you remember that one who bit the other man's ear? That game is brutality itself; I don't know what they are teaching young children, especially boys.

"I hope parents don't let young children watch the boxing match, and anyway, children should be in bed by that time. The younger children shouldn't watch that type of brutality. I think they should be at least sixteen years old before parents allow them to watch boxing matches on TV.

"When boxing starts, I will go to the other room to finish off those curtains I was stitching for Annette. After that, it would be all hands on deck for the wedding day plans."

Malc said; "Well, you have more than six months to plan for the big day."

"Yes, I know that but there is quite a lot to prepare for the wedding. I wonder how many bridesmaids Annette wants. It's not just the Minister we have to plan the celebrations with seamstresses and bakers too. Annette is lucky both Wilma and I are dressmakers, it's very expensive to buy the dresses nowadays."

Malc and Dorothy sat down at the kitchen table for supper. After they ate, Dorothy made some fried dumplings and tri-tri cakes from the mixtures she had prepared earlier. Then about forty minutes later, Dorothy was tidying the kitchen and washing the dishes.

♣♣♣♣♣

Ruby Starskey

There was a knock at the front door Malc went to check, and when he opened the door it was one of their neighbours.

Malc said; "Hello Ruby, what's up?"

Ms Starskey lives in a little rundown shack with six children. And her partner Cliff Matthews, a petty thief, is in and out of jail; he is currently resided at her majesty's pleasure.

"Mr Melrose, my roof blow right off my house in the storm; would you mind if I used your phone? I need somewhere to stay. I don't know where I'm going to get the money from to repair my house."

"Come in you can use the phone but don't stay too long; phone bill na' cheap!" Malc', why are you so rude to our neighbour; remarked Dorothy.

Ruby walked to the phone, she dialled the number, and her brother Dawnis answered the phone after a few rings.

"Hello bruv, you okay? I'm at my neighbour Mr Melrose".

"What has the storm done to you?"

Dawnis said; "We is all right, man; just some banana trees blow down. But apart from that, we okay."

"I'm not so lucky bruv; my house roof got damaged in the storm galvanise roof garn and water everywhere, even the bed wet. *I'm begging you please; bruv*! Could we stay with you until the roof gets repaired?"

"Repaired? How you going to manage that without money? *I would bring the truck to pick you up, but me karn come tonight!*"

"Lord Jesus and I don't have enough money to catch bus to country!"

"Ask your neighbour to keep you till tomorrow; said Dawnis". Dawnis continued; "after all, I feel like I have some connections with the Melrose because Gideon is marrying their daughter and I am looking after Gideon's dad farmland."

"Hold on a minute bruv; said Ruby". Excuse me, Mr Melrose; me bruv say he can't come tonight to pick us up; do you mind putting us up for the night?"

Dorothy said; "It's the least we could do; tell your brother you can stay here until tomorrow."

Ms Starskey returned to her house, an hour later she came back with her six children in tow: Desmond, Leroy, Kenrick, Godwin, Aaron, and carrying her six-month-old baby son Cedric. They each carried a sack, perhaps with all their personal belongings.

Malc opened the door for Ruby and her sons. Ruby said; "Thanks, I'm very grateful."

Dorothy was standing right behind her husband and he asked; "You all hungry?"

The boys all shouted, "Yes!" "As if little boys would refuse food; remarked Malc"

Dorothy said; "Lucky for you children, I just made some fried dumplings and tri-tri cakes. Shall I make the boys some ovaltine?"

"The boys would eat anything and everything, even Cedric is not a fussy eater. He would eat the tri-tri cakes but the fried dumplings might choke him; he is a bit too young. Do you have any bread?"

"Yes, he could have bread with a drink of ovaltine"

"Thanks, Mrs Melrose."

All of Ruby's family now gathered in the big kitchen. Mr Melrose walked over to the dining table and bent down to adjust something under the table. He said, "Let me just expand the table; we keep it small for more space, as it's only four of us who uses it regularly." But Annette will be moving out soon when she gets married. Then he fetched some more chairs he kept under the stairs cupboard.

Eight chairs in total were just enough to seat the family, as Cedric sat on his mother's lap. There was nothing left on any of the plates. Ruby was right; her children were hearty eaters. The children were clean and tidy and already wearing their pyjamas when they arrived.

An hour later after supper, Dorothy said, "Come; let me show you where the children will sleep. I'm afraid there is not enough room; some will have to sleep on the floor."

Ruby said, "That's okay, I have three sleeping bags with me; they didn't get wet in the storm."

They all went upstairs to the bedrooms; Dorothy led the way. Ruby looked around and said, "This room is quite big; six of them would fit in here easily."

Then Dorothy walked over to the other bedroom and said to Ruby, "You can sleep in this room with baby Cedric." It was much smaller with a single bed; it was the spare bedroom.

"Thanks again for everything."

"You are welcome! Here are some bath towels."

Ruby said, "Oh, that's okay, they are all washed and ready for bed, just need to brush their teeth now. They won't give you any trouble. I would make sure of that. I have my little radio; don't worry, I won't play it loudly."

"Okay, I have some curtains to finish off in my sewing room downstairs, and Malc will be watching the boxing match."

"Oh yes, me did plan to watch it too. If I could settle Cedric to bed, would Mr Melrose mind me watching the boxing match?"

Dorothy said, "I'm sure he would be happy for you to join him."

The boys were busy brushing their teeth. Ruby went to the other bedroom to try and calm Cedric to sleep, and within ten minutes he was fast asleep. Ruby stood up from the bed, walked out quietly, and closed the door. She went to the other bedroom, where the boys were getting into their sleeping bags.

"Leroy, you just behave yourself and stop provoking your brother."

Leroy said, "Mammy, I don't want to sleep with Aaron; *he does mek too much noise!*"

"Leroy; please explain to me how do you know that Aaron is snoring if you are fast asleep?"

Leroy said; "well; because it's so loud it wakes me out of my sleep."

"You don't need to worry Leroy; you won't hear him tonight if you sleep soundly. Good night, children . . . sleep tight . . . love you all."

"Love you more, Mammy," replied the boys.

Ruby went downstairs and knocked on the lounge door, where Mr Melrose was in an animated state, he was shouting and pointing towards the TV, telling the boxer he was supporting to float like a butterfly, like the great Mohammad Ali used to say. Malc turned to Ruby and ushered her to sit down.

Malc said; "Do you like boxing too, Ruby?"

"Yes, Mr Melrose, I had planned to watch this match; have I missed much?"

"No, only ten minutes; would you like a beer?"

"Yes please."

"Please help yourself, he said, pointing to the tray on the coffee table in front of him."

Ruby took a beer and opened it.

The two boxers' names are Basil Sampson, a Negro, and Duga Han, an Indian; explained Malc.

Ruby shouted; "come on, Basil, you can't let that coolie beat you! Show him how strong you are!"

"The two of boxers are the same height, but Basil looks fitter, more muscular. Basil does a lot of weight lifting and mountain hiking. He has his own personal trainer and a nutritionist telling him what to eat; not too much fried chicken is involved in his diet, you know!"

"Oh, that one was below the belt; remarked Malc".

Ruby said; "come on, Basil, keep focused."

Ruby turned to Mr Melrose and said, "The coolie nearly knocked him out, but Basil good though!"

"Han won that round but Sampson is leading. They have another six rounds to go if someone doesn't get knocked out."

Ruby said; "Han's knees look weak."

Malc said; "maybe Sampson will get to him in the next round."

And the bell went just in time for Han to take a rest.

Looking weak and exhausted, the boxers walked to their corners; there was only two minutes between for them to rest each rounds. Sampson's lip was bleeding and Han had a deep cut over his left eye. Both men were having their wounds cleaned and then covered with plaster. Any boxers who suffered an open wound while competing had to cover the bleeding wounds with plaster.

The bell went and both men jumped to their feet and began sparring. Sampson struck a blow but missed Han; Han moved in closer to Sampson, striking several blows to Sampson's chest. Sampson waited for clearance and struck Han just above his wounded left eye. Han fell to the floor; the referee started the count but Han was out cold; his trainer threw a towel in the ring to end the match. Sampson's corner raised their arms in victory.

Mr Melrose and Ruby jumped up from their seats victorious; Dorothy walked in just in time to see a doctor assisting Han. After a few minutes Han was on his feet; he walked over to Sampson and shook his hand. They embraced in a professional gesture to the ecstatic crowd of Sampson's fans cheering.

Ruby said; "Mr Melrose, how much money is the winner getting?"

"Sampson is a wealthy man now; he gets $250,000."

"My word, that was not bad for half an hour punching in a boxing ring; do women box, Mr Melrose?"

"Of course, there are women in Europe and America competing in boxing matches. Mohammad Ali's daughter is a boxer."

"Ah . . . . true?" remarked Ruby.

Ruby finished her last drop of beer and then thanked Mr Melrose, she said good night to Dorothy and Malc. She went to use the bathroom and brushed her teeth; she put her nightie on and climbed into bed next to her baby son Cedric. He was fast asleep.

♣♣♣♣♣

Early the next morning, the sound of cockerels crowing woke Cedric; he raised his head and started crying.

Ruby sat up and said to her son, "Hello sweetheart. Did you sleep well?"

He responded in his own baby language, smiling up at his mammy. Then suddenly Ruby realised she wasn't at home. "Oh dear, you need some tea but we not at home."

Ruby thought quietly and then said, "Anyway, Mrs Melrose showed me last night where everything was in the kitchen to make breakfast. And she did say we could use the leftover fried dumplings for breakfast."

Ruby got out of bed, lifted Cedric, and went downstairs quietly; she was careful not to wake her hosts and the boys. She went straight to the kitchen and made some tea for Cedric.

She turned her transistor radio on; by that time it was nearly six o'clock. The news came on and the radio announcer read out the news items. He said the Prime Minister was on that morning's agenda. First on the list was the boxing result from last night's match, followed by the news of the storm which devastated the island a day ago.

The radio announcer, Angus Donlap, said, "Good morning listeners! On this glorious morning after the storm, I have here with me a special guest: Prime Minister Vivian Agare." There was a short silence, and then the Prime Minister read a statement:

> *"Good morning listeners, on behalf of my government and members of the opposition parliamentary party, I must say: thank God; we were lucky during the storm last night. No fatalities were reported. But we have suffered catastrophic damage to homes and our agricultural crops.*
>
> *We have set aside contingency funds to help the poorest in our community whose homes were damaged by the ferocious storm yesterday.*
>
> *We have a team of carpenters who would visit villages to assess the storm damaged homes. Our relief assistants will decide what is needed to get our citizens back into their homes.*
>
> *This may take a few weeks but we are starting this urgent project from today, as we can appreciate the urgency of this matter. We wouldn't want to prolong the burden on families, neighbours, or friends giving shelter.*
>
> *So our main aim is to help all poor and needy victims of storm damaged homes as quickly as possible.*
>
> *God bless you all"*.

♣♣♣♣♣

Ruby said; "My goodness, our Prime Minister is the best!"
Dorothy entered the kitchen just in time to hear Ruby's remark.
Dorothy said; "good morning Ruby," but Ruby was so excited she responded, "Mrs Melrose, I can't believe what I've just heard on the radio: the Prime Minister just been talking; he is going to fix my roof!"

"What? He's going to fix your roof? Are you joking?"

Ruby said; "no, he was just talking on the radio, saying a team of carpenters going to repair poor people's storm damaged homes."

Dorothy laughed and said, "General election is imminent; what a voting gimmick. Well! But I suppose that's gratifying for people who need urgent help."

"Oh that reminds me, my brother is coming to take us up to the country. But I think I would just allow the boys up to stay with our family until my roof is fixed. I need to stay at home and find out who would repair my house urgently. I need to get it done quick sharp, as I don't want my boys to miss a day in school."

By 8:30 that morning, everyone was up and Ruby made sure the boys were cleaned and fed before her brother arrived. Later on Ruby and Dorothy sat in the kitchen, and they told Malc the good news. Ruby told him that she would be getting help from the government to repair her storm damaged roof.

Malc said; "if you could find out who you need to contact, I'm certain Gideon can help. He could get your galvanised roof up in a couple of hours. If you wait on a government team to help, it might take a little longer."

Ruby said; "oh, listen": she turned the volume up on her little transistor radio.

It was broadcasting a storm relief number for anyone (the very poor) to contact a local builder assigned by the government to carry out repair work to damaged homes.

Ruby wrote the number down on an old piece of paper and showed it to Mr Melrose.

"This is Gideon's number," he said.

Ruby said; "oh hallelujah, it is true that God really does provide."

"Let me ring Gideon now so that he could put you at the top of his queue. I'm certain he would have your roof repaired before the end of today, hopefully."

Mr Melrose dialled the number; he got through to Gideon after three rings.

"Hello son; good morning."

"Oh good morning Dad; said Gideon."

Malc and Gideon were very courteous to each other; there was a special father/son bond between them. And Malc, being friends with

Gideon's parents, had known his future son-in-law ever since he was born.

Malc said to Gideon, "Ruby stayed with us overnight."

"What, the woman with seven kids?"

Malc said; "six, actually; this morning Ruby was listening to the radio and she heard that the government is helping poor families to repair storm damaged roofs."

"Oh yes, yes, I'm just about to collect some galvanised roofing at the hardware store in town."

"Oh good son anybody call you yet?"

"Yes, I have just one family so far but I imagine there will be hundreds more."

Malc said; "Please can you put Ruby Starskey down on your home repair list?"

"Of course, I can appreciate the urgency, or that woman and her boys would eat you out of home and country if you have to keep them another night. Tell Ruby her house roof would get done today. I can't say what time but she is second on my list."

"Wonderful; see you soon, son."

"All right, bye."

Malc hung up the phone and said, "Ruby, your home should be ready today."

Ruby said; "I feel lucky today." She raised her arms and added, "Oh God is great! My brother already left home; he was coming into town anyway . . . so he is not coming on a wasted journey. Besides, I'm excited to see him!"

A few hours later that morning a truck pulled up outside the Melrose's front yard; the boys were outside playing a ball game.

Aaron ran into the kitchen, where Ruby was washing dishes; he said, "Mammy, Mammy, Uncle Dawnis is outside."

She ran towards the front door and shouted, "Hello bruv! Long time no see; how you doing?"

Dawnis said; "yes I'm good, Sis."

Ruby stepped back to admire her brother; she said, "You put on some weight, man?"

Dawnis said; "yes, I do a lot of body building weight training. I go to Angus Bella's gym on the main road."

"Oh, you should consider boxing as a career; you have the body for it."

"Yes, I was thinking the same thing as I watched the match on TV last night."

"Me too, and Mr Melrose was telling me that boxers can become millionaires."

"Sis, do you know it's the same thing I was thinking, but I wonder if I've missed my chance. I'm going to be twenty soon."

"What? Twenty is not old, my bruv. You should explore the possibilities of becoming a boxer."

"Yes, you are right; the banana industry is doomed; most of our bananas trees fell during the storm, so money is going to be tight."

Ruby said; "we certainly need to think of other means to survive." Then she turned to her brother and continued, "Bruv, you won't believe my luck, I am going to get some help to repair my house roof. The prime minister was on the radio this morning. The government is helping poor people like me whose homes got damaged in the storm. Mr Melrose's son-in-law is one of the companies assigned to carry out the repair work. So my house will be repaired today."

"That is excellent news, Sis."

Dawnis reached for his wallet and took some money out; he gave it to Ruby and said, "Here, Daddy say to give you this."

It was $100.

"Wow . . . . the boys need quite a bit for school. Oh, I'm so blessed . . . you know Dad and my father-in-law Freddy Matthews are my saviours; I do pray for them every day!"

"Anyway Sis, I'm going to love you and leave you; I've got some business to take care of in town. Boys, see you soon! I will come and fetch you to spend some time in the country when you are next on school holidays in December."

Ruby said; "but that's three months away, bruv, just a matter of weeks."

"All right, Sis, I'll see you guys soon!" He jumped into his truck, turned the engine on, and roared off towards Kingstown, waving back at his sister and nephews. Even baby Cedric was waving!

Ruby turned to the boys and said; "right, boys, let's give Mr and Mrs Melrose some space. Go and get your belongings and let's go back to the house; we have someone coming today to repair the roof."

Leroy said; "Mammy at least it not raining now."

"Yes, we are going to have a dry and sunny day today," answered his mother.

Ruby said; "The roof will be in tip-top shape by Monday, and today is Saturday, so you have enough time to do your homework. Leroy, you need to finish off that book you were reading. Tomorrow is Sunday; we have to go to church and give thanks to God."

As the children got nearer to the house the brothers decided to race to the front door. Desmond and Leroy were first on the doorstep.

Desmond said to Leroy, "Mammy has the key, and look how far back she is!"

The boys waited a few minutes but it seemed longer to them. As soon as Ruby opened the door, the boys rushed indoors. Ruby seated Cedric in his high chair. Her father had made the high chair when his first grandson was born. Then she went straight to her bedroom; talking aloud, she said, "God, please help me to get a house like the Melrose's for me and my sons. I promise you I won't ask for anything else; thank you Lord."

Almost instantly, she heard someone shouting her name, followed by the boys shouting too.

"Mammy, Mammy, Mr LeBoun is here!"

Ruby said; "God, that was quick," as she rushed to the door step. Gideon was standing in the yard, surrounded by her five sons.

"Oh hi Ruby," said Gideon.

"Hello Gideon, it's good to see you, man. I wasn't expecting you until later on today," Ruby said.

Gideon said; "The first house didn't need much done to it, just a few sheets of galvanised roofing to replace. I could start yours right away."

"Okay, thanks."

Gideon and his assistant began to unload the sheets of galvanised roofing. He said to Ruby, "Can I ask you to keep the children at a distance? Better still, it might be safer to take them somewhere."

"That's okay, I have to go and buy a few groceries."

Godwin said; "Mammy, can we go to Gary's house?"

"Yes, the older boys can go, but Aaron and Cedric have to come to the shop with me."

Ruby and the boys all set off together, as Gary's house was the same direction as the shop. When they arrived at the Pope's front gate, Ruby shouted, "Jenny, are you home?"

Gary answered; "yes, Mammy is washing some clothes in the back yard."

Ruby walked around to the back; as soon as Jenny saw her, she stopped what she was doing and said, "Girl, are you okay?"

"Yes babe; the Lord is great; my roof is being repaired as we speak."

"You mean with the government funds?" asked Jenny.

"Yes, Gideon LeBoun is repairing the roof right now."

Jenny said; "oh, the man who is marrying Annette Melrose?"

"The same one;" said Ruby.

"You are lucky;" remarked Jenny.

Ruby said, "This time yesterday I was pondering what to do. It really is true that we shouldn't worry about anything, because every little thing is going to be all right. Bob Marley really was a prophet; every lyric he ever wrote came true."

Ruby sat on the back wall and Jenny continued to wash her laundry. She was nearly finished and poured water in the sink to rinse off the clothes.

Then five minutes later, she was hanging the clothes on the line down the back garden. Ruby jumped down from the wall where she sat and began to help Jenny hang the clothes on the line, and they finished in no time.

Ruby always carried Cedric strapped to her chest; it allowed her to do other things with her hands: carrying shopping, and so on.

Jenny said, "Let us go inside; my favourite soap is coming on shortly. I've made a big pot of soup; there is enough for everybody. Even Cedric could have a bowl of the soup."

Ruby helped Jenny to serve the soup into bowls. Then Jenny called her son Gary, he was her only child, and her husband is Dale, who owned a stall in Kingstown market, selling fish.

There were not enough chairs around the table in the kitchen, so the older boys sat on the back door steps. Jenny gave the boys homemade lemonade with ice, and the ladies drank a bottle of beer while they sat watching their favourite American soap on TV, *Days of Our Lives*.

By the time Ruby left Jenny's house, it was two o'clock; she went to the shop quickly, with Cedric and Aaron in tow. The older boys stayed behind to play ball games with Gary. Ruby went straight to her house on her way back from the grocery store.

When she got close to the front gate, she saw the galvanised roof was back on securely; it was a happy sight for Ruby. She placed her groceries on the ground and raised her hand up in the air. Looking up to the sky, she thanked God again, not forgetting the Prime Minister of St Vincent and the Grenadines for the help and support.

Ruby prayed, "Lord, I was so stressed worrying about money. I was thinking, where am I going to get the money from to fix my home? And with all the hungry mouths I have to feed—I have limited funds. Praise the good Lord; Mr LeBoun has done a good job."

Then she looked at the boys and said, "My sons, we are the luckiest people today! A few days ago I was so stressed, wondering when my home would be fixed to live in again."

Ruby added, "I don't care what people say about our Prime Minister, he is a good man."

Ruby was clasping her hands when she looked up to the sky. She said, "This is my prayer for the Prime Minister."

She began to pray:

> *"Thank you, Lord, for everything I got my house roof repaired and money from Daddy in my purse."*

Ruby felt the need to continue praying:

> *"Heavenly father, thank you very much for everything and all the help I received today. A special thanks for our Prime Minister, I know that it is not an easy job, but whatever work he is doing, help him to continue to do it well. He is a good leader, and it's not just him leading the Country. I pray for the other members of our government; give them the wisdom and understanding to work together as one in unity and dedication. Amen!"*

After praying, Ruby turned to her son and said, "Aaron, let's go inside; you could help me to tidy up the house. It's only four o'clock; if I do some washing, they will be dry by seven o'clock. Please, can you fetch me the laundry clothes to wash?

"But we go to bed at eight, Mammy," Aaron said.

"Yes, that's correct. Please go and clean your shoes for church tomorrow."

"Okay, Mammy;" replied Aaron.

He ran off towards the bedroom and returned to the kitchen with the laundry. Then he sat on the door step with the shoe shining kit and began to clean his shoes.

His mother stood at the sink just outside the kitchen door, it took thirty minutes to wash every garment, and then she went down the back garden and hung the laundry out on the clothes line, piece by piece. While she was washing the clothes, Cedric was taking his daily siesta, even though it was a bit later in the day than normal.

As soon as Ruby walked into the living room, Cedric raised his head and began to cry.

Ruby said; "good timing; are you hungry?"

Cedric stretched his arms out, and Ruby lifted him high and kissed him on the forehead. She realised Cedric's diaper smelled foul and needed changing; she went to the bathroom and changed his diaper, and then took him into the kitchen.

"Would you like some farley's rusk?"

She reached for the biscuits in the cupboard and then broke one in half. She gave Aaron a piece and Cedric the other half with a cup of orange juice. She sat Cedric in his high chair, turned the radio on, and then began to peel some potatoes.

She was giving the boys their favourite: fried potato chips with hot dog sausages and mushy peas. She told Aaron to go and fetch his brothers from next door because supper would be ready in thirty minutes. Ruby knew you had to eat chips as soon as they were ready or they'd go cold quickly.

A few minutes later, Ruby could hear the boys coming into the yard. Desmond was first to the kitchen door.

She said; "wash your hands please, and put the crockery on the table. There is a jug of lemon juice in the fridge; put it out on the table with some glasses."

By that time all the boys were seated, hands washed, ready to eat their favourite meal. After supper, Ruby ordered the boys to clean their shoes for tomorrow and then go and shower.

"You might as well put your pyjamas on because it will be dark soon almost bedtime."

"Can we watch TV after we bathe, Mammy?"

"Yes, but after eight o'clock it's my time."

Chapter 2

The LeBoun Family Dinner

Laverne is Wilma and Josh's youngest child, she had telephoned her mother from work to tell her to prepare supper for twelve people; her brothers, Sam, James, and Gideon, and their partners were coming for a Saturday evening get-together.

Laverne's mum Wilma asked, "Shall I cook a casserole?"

"Oh that would be nice with mutton," replied Laverne.

Laverne's mum Wilma said, "Yes, I have some meat I bought in town yesterday. Okay, see you soon, sweetheart!"

Sam is married to Patsie, and they have a two-year-old son, Danny. James is married to Marcia, and Gideon is engaged to Annette Melrose. Laverne's is dating Bradley Grayson, and she still lives at home with her parents.

Earlier that day on Saturday morning, Wilma had gone to the kitchen to bake a cake. She had planned to make a nice sponge fruit cake, but when she checked the cupboard she didn't have any mixed dried fruits left.

So instead she decided to make two chocolate cakes laced with rum; it was one of her children's favourite cakes. Wilma didn't need to measure anything; she was so familiar with the list of ingredients, it was easy for her. She used enough ingredients to make two big sponge cakes because she knew how much her children enjoyed her cakes. An hour later, her kitchen was filled with the delicious aroma from the chocolate rum cakes.

Wilma kept looking at the two chocolate cakes on the cooling rack. They looked so delicious she just couldn't resist the temptation, so she reached for a knife and cut herself a slice. She ate the cake with a glass of strawberry juice with ice.

Later on, she heard a vehicle pull up into the front yard. Wilma stood up and walked to the window; she pulled opened the curtain and saw Sam. Patsie lifted her son Danny from his car seat. Laverne opened the front door and greeted her nephew: "Hello, Danny," and then they went to the kitchen. Sam walked in with James followed Marcia and Patsie. Then Josh and Bradley join the family in the kitchen.

Laverne put Danny down and he ran straight to his grandmother, who was stooping with arms open to greet him. She lifted him high, hugged him, and kissed him. Laverne and Bradley took one glance at the chocolate cake, and without hesitating, Laverne reached for the knife and sliced several portions. Danny was so excited; he loved to eat anything sweet. Laverne said, "Yum, um, this is delicious!"

Josh said, "My wife makes delicious cakes, good enough for the Queen of England."

Everybody laughed!

James said, "Dad you're so comical!"

There were two sour sops in the fruit bowl on the dining table. Laverne examined them and told her mother that they were ripe and ready to use. Laverne said, "Oh, can we have soursop juice with dinner?"

Her mum replied, "I haven't made soursop juice since you children were teenagers."

Laverne said, "That's only a few years ago, Mum! I'll make the soursop juice."

She walked over to the sink and squeezed open the ripe fruits. She used a big spoon to lift the white sticky flesh into a big jug, taking extra care to remove every black seed. She used a strainer to squeeze the juice from the soursop flesh and then added a tin of evaporated milk and sugar to taste.

Laverne poured some of the soursop juice into a small glass and gave it to Danny. She said to Patsie, "If he drinks it, you know it's good."

Danny tasted a little of the juice and then he drank it until the glass was empty.

Laverne said, "That's our answer, the juice is good."

Danny put the cup on the dining table and ran straight to his dad, who was watching TV with his granddad.

Wilma shouted from the kitchen that dinner was ready; Josh jumped to his feet, followed by James and Sam. Laverne stood just outside the kitchen and the hallway at the bottom of the stairs and shouted to her brother; she said, "Gideon, dinner is ready!"

She waited for a minute. Then she saw Annette, and Gideon was close behind her, with one arm around Annette's shoulder.

She was admiring the romantic couple, Annette and her brother Gideon. Laverne said, "I don't know . . . you two lovebirds."

Gideon said, "And you are not romantic, Sis?"

She knew he was right; she smiled broadly and walked to the kitchen, with the two lovebirds following behind her.

When everyone was seated at the dining table, it was customary for the family to say a short prayer before each meal. Everyone clasped their hands together and Josh prayed, "Lord, we thank you for what we are about to receive. Amen!" After dinner they all thanked their mother for the delicious meal, and good company too, remarked dad Josh. "Mum is an excellent chef," replied Sam.

Gideon and Sam helped to tidy up the kitchen. Laverne and Bradley helped to put away the pots and plates in the cupboards. Gideon and Sam worked in the building trade they busy talking about work. Sam did brickwork and Gideon built homes so they had a lot in common; conversations with those two were never boring.

After the children left Wilma and Josh sat down to watch TV but they fell asleep within a few minutes.

Chapter 3

Meeting with Rev. Monsolo

After Sunday service, both set of families joined the minister to discuss wedding plans for Annette and Gideon's special day. It was the meeting they had postponed during the night of the storm. Firstly, the minister wanted to know how big the wedding group would be.

Annette had a notepad with all of her wedding plans written out.

She said, "I am having three bridesmaids, and my big sister Betsie is my maid of honour."

Gideon said, "I will have three ushers, and my brother Sam will be my best man."

Rev. Monsolo said, "I prefer the groom and best man to arrive at least thirty minutes before the bride. And the bride must arrive five minutes before the schedule wedding service. But I have never known a bride to arrive on time."

Everyone laughed.

Rev. Monsolo said, "Annette, I'm not saying that you should be very late. That wouldn't be good for any of us, as weddings can be a stressful time. We must try and minimise stress and make it an exciting and enjoyable day. We will announce the marriage notice two weeks before the big day in church service."

Mrs Melrose said, "As the parents of the bride and groom, will we go into the vestry to sign the register?"

Rev. Monsolo said, "Yes, we normally allow parents to witness the signing of the register. The vestry is not big enough to fit the whole bridal party and photographers. So the bridesmaids can wait in the church hallway just outside the vestry."

Mrs Melrose said, "What about hymns?"

Rev. Monsolo said, "Oh yes; I have some songs especially for weddings, as well as Scripture readings. But some couples like to play one of their favourite love songs in the background after the matrimonial service ends."

Annette said, "I quite like the Bob Marley's song, "One love."

Rev. Monsolo said, "You have exactly eight months, and I wish you guys all the best planning this wonderful event. The longer you have to organise everything, the better the results. Do you have any more questions?"

There was a moment of silence, and then Gideon said, "I think that's all for now, Rev. Monsolo."

The minister said, "Perfect; just call me if you have any more questions. About two weeks from the wedding date, I would like the bridal party to come to a rehearsal prior to the wedding day. That includes the bride, groom, bridesmaids and ushers, best man, and father of the bride. We will rehearse the procedures to follow on the big day, okay?"

"Yes Rev."

They all stood up and the minister bid them good evening.

The families were walking out of the church gate when they heard a loud bang by the roadside. It was a mini bus and a big truck, which collided as they approached a blind corner about fifty yards from the church. The men ran ahead of the ladies to see if they could help in any way.

Gideon was first at the scene; the mini bus driver looked unconscious, and blood was pouring from his head. The big truck took most of the impact, but the driver was able to climb out of the truck; he was limping and had hurt his ankle.

By that time the minister was standing with the ladies at the crash scene. He tried to comfort Mrs Melrose and Mrs LeBoun, because they were in shock. Then he walked over to check on the passengers, who stood dazed and shaken.

One of the women was shouting and screaming at the mini bus driver; she said, "You was driving too fast, speeding, and the damn music playing in the bus was too loud!"

The minister said, "Okay, okay, let us thank God that no one has lost their life. We need to call the emergency service; the driver needs medical assistance. He is badly hurt."

Rev. Monsolo turned to the truck driver and told him to sit and rest his hurt ankle. "It could be broken," he remarked. "If you try and walk or stand on it, it might make things worse."

The minister went back to the house and rang for an ambulance. The assistant told Rev. Monsolo it would take thirty minutes to get to the crash scene, adding, "If someone could take the injured passengers to Kingstown General Hospital, it would help enormously. In the meantime, I will request accident service to come and clear the road. And a police officer is on his way to make sure the road is secure and open for traffic again."

The Melrose and LeBoun families realised they wouldn't be able to drive through the route they came, as the two collided vehicles were blocking the way. So they decided to drive in the opposite direction and took another route home. It took twice as long, but it was better than waiting until the police cleared the road for traffic again. Gideon offered to take the two injured drivers to the Hospital, and Rev. Monsolo said, "God bless you son that's very charitable of you".

♣♣♣♣♣

On Sunday morning, the Melrose and LeBoun families were up early to go to Church. It was the first Sunday since they'd witnessed the road accident shortly after meeting to talk about wedding plans with Rev. Monsolo.

Wilma and Josh were having breakfast in the kitchen; he told her that the truck driver who was involved in the accident was from Springtown. He had broken his ankle and he would be laid up from work for a while.

Josh went on to say, "All these reckless drivers need to take heed; they drive like lunatics on the roads. The mini bus was carrying passengers from Clay Village, travelling to Kingstown when it collided with the truck. At least there were no fatalities, but I can't understand why people drive at such speed, sometimes turning blind corners at excessive speed. This is a huge problem and reckless driving kills innocent people too frequently."

Chapter 4

Wedding Outfits

Dorothy and Wilma had planned to go shopping to purchase the fabrics they needed to make the bridesmaid dresses. Annette had chosen powder blue for her bridesmaid dresses, gold for her mother, and peach for her mother-in-law's outfit. The men would wear grey safari suits and light colour blue shirts.

Early that morning, Wilma collected Dorothy, who lived a few blocks from her house, to go into town. As they approached the main road, the traffic up the hill wasn't moving.

Dorothy said to Wilma, "It's getting worse; there are too many cars in St Vincent."

"We could talk . . . our family owns more than one vehicle, truck, and cars combined; replied Wilma."

Dorothy said, "In our days we could only rely on the public transport service, and the seats on the buses were far from comfortable."

The traffic was still at a standstill, and Dorothy was looking at the views across the airport, which overlooked the blue sea and far beyond. As they sat in traffic feeling bored Dorothy remarked; "the sea is stretched across the wide area like a blue carpet and the water looks solid, as if you could walk on it."

"It's a good thing we are not going anywhere in a hurry, because that would really be frustrating; remarked Dorothy."

A few minutes later, they began to move again; the gridlock traffic had cleared, and five minutes later they arrived in Kingstown.

"Let's go and buy some fresh fish before we do anything else," said Wilma."

Dorothy said, "Yes, you're right; let's go to Dale's stall. He can keep the fish in his fridge, because if we leave it in the car, the fish could rot from the heat."

Dale was Jenny Pope's husband, they are Ruby's neighbours.

Dorothy and Wilma arrived at the market in Bay Street; it was busy with vendors and customers. They went straight to Dale's stall, and he had various fish on display for sale. Dorothy noticed a big tuna and lots of red snappers, and he had the tiny sardines better known as tri-tri on the Island.

Wilma spoke first; she ordered some red snappers.

Then it was Dorothy's turn; she asked Dale to weigh one of the big tuna fish.

Dale said to Dorothy, "Mrs Melrose, this is expensive fish, you know?"

"Weigh it please," she said, "and let me decide, okay?"

Dale weighed the fish; it was worth $50 but he charged Dorothy $40.

"Please keep them in the fridge until later," Dorothy said. "We will collect them when we finish shopping."

"Let me put our names on the bags," said Wilma.

Dale also placed a notice on the bag: "Sold."

The ladies said, "That's good, thanks. See you later!"

Just outside the market there were vendors selling vegetables and they sat on the wooden boxes that they used to carry the vegetables. They sat all day long, watching and waiting for buyers to take pity and hoping for a few sales. Some vendors sat quietly, but others made sure no one passed by without attracting their attention, trying to sell them something.

Dorothy and Wilma left the market plaza and returned to the car to leave the goods they'd bought. Then Wilma needed some cash at the bank. As they entered the bank, Wilma said, "Oh, no, we will be here for a while, the queue was very long."

Dorothy said, "You wait in the queue; I need to go to the bakery."

"Please bring me some cakes you know the ones I buy regularly, and one chicken roti, and a bottle of mauby for lunch," said Wilma."

Dorothy shopped for thirty minutes, and when she returned to the bank, there were only two people waiting in the queue ahead of Wilma.

Dorothy said, "What a surprise, I was expecting to eat my roti standing right here next to you!"

"It is good progress the staff at the bank are working more efficiently; it should only take fifteen minutes max two people and then it's my turn to be served."

Dorothy said, "That wasn't too long; we'll be out of here shortly."

"We could go back to the car and eat lunch; said Wilma. Less than ten minutes later, Dorothy and Wilma left the bank. They walked to the car and ate lunch Wilma was first to climb into the car; she sat on the front seat and said, "Jesus, it's like an oven in here. I'm certain you could fry an egg on this dashboard!"

Dorothy climbed in the seat next to her friend and said, "Jeees, the hot seat is melting my tal-le-la!"

Wilma said, "Ha ha ha, our baby house is burning!"

"Stop your slackness," remarked Dorothy.

Wilma said, "You started it." They both laughed.

Dorothy said; "but wait a minute; did you ever wonder about all the names we use for male and female private parts?"

"Yes, let's see how many names we can come up with; female genitals first."

They came up with pundin, tal-le-la, baby house, porkey, pussy, pum-pum, cunt, kat, mampoo, punnanee, quartet, and cunny.

"My great-grandma used to call it tarba-larba," said Dorothy. "And of course the correct universal name is vagina."

Then they listed the names for male genitals: tollow, wood, private, manhood, dick, cock, bamboo, willie, bud, sausage, and of course penis. Both women were in hysterics; "What a life," remarked Wilma.

They continued eating lunch in silence.

Before they left for the store, Wilma said, "What if we can't get the right shade of blue Annette wants for the bridesmaid dresses?"

Dorothy said, "Then we have to go right back to the drawing board and choose a different colour."

"Annette has set her heart on powder blue. At least we don't have to worry about her bridal gown; that is coming ready made from Annette's Aunty Cynthia in America."

They got out of the car and walked towards the boutique store. Wilma stopped to look at some jewellery; she saw some bracelets and thought they would make lovely bridesmaid gifts.

Wilma said, "Look Dorothy, we could get four of these for the girls."

"Oh yes, they're nice."

They asked the assistant how much the bracelets were; she told them $30 each. Wilma and Dorothy agreed to split the costs and purchased two bracelets each.

Dorothy and Wilma went to the next floor at the boutique store, where they stocked fabrics in abundance for sale. They had all shades of blue, but none of the fabrics came close to the powder blue Annette wanted for the bridesmaid dresses. But all was not in vain though, as Dorothy and Wilma saw gold and peach fabrics to make their wedding outfits. After they paid for the gold and peach fabrics for their dresses, thread, zips, and sequins, Wilma remarked, "At least this is half our mission accomplished."

Dorothy said; "But what colour shoes are we going to wear?"

Wilma suggested black shoes and handbags. "That should be easy to co-ordinate the colours; in fact, we both have black shoes and handbags."

They paid for the goods and then left the store. They headed towards the other boutique store in pursuit of the perfect powder blue fabric for the bridesmaid dresses. As soon as they entered the store, they noticed a powder blue fabric.

Wilma said; "Oh, this would do nicely."

Dorothy agreed; they bought the fabric, thread, and zip for the dresses, and a lovely bit of white lace as part of the design. The bridesmaids would dress in white shoes, and the bride would carry red and white roses with a little green sago for her bouquet.

Finally, at the end of the shopping spree they walked back to Dale's and collected the fish they had bought earlier, and then they headed home. They arrived back home in twenty minutes, as the traffic was flowing smoothly.

Wilma and Dorothy suggested they start dressmaking Wednesday, and they organised two assistants to help stitch the dresses. Dorothy assigned seamstress Paulina Pretty, and Eloise Scubie would work with Wilma.

Dorothy said; "Let's get the bridesmaid dresses done first then we'll do our outfits."

"Okay, anyway we are four of the best seamstresses on the island of St Vincent."

"This wedding is going to be like the American TV show 'Dynasty.'" Of course they both laughed.

♣♣♣♣♣

On a bright sunny Wednesday morning, Dorothy and Wilma planned to begin work sewing the bridesmaid outfits. Wilma arrived at Dorothy's home to begin the first stages of dressmaking. Firstly, they arranged the fabrics on a big dining table and used the same dress patterns from some previous outfits they had used for another wedding. They pinned the patterns onto the fabrics and began to cut the shapes out. It was an effortless task, and Dorothy and Wilma finished cutting out the dress patterns in no time.

Dorothy decided to take a lunch break around noon, so she went to the kitchen to fix a meal. She was listening to a talk show program on the radio. It was a lively program for listeners to phone in and asked questions about medical problems. A doctor was on hand to answer medical problems or concerns from the general public.

The program's first caller mentioned that she had read in a magazine article that broccoli can prevent a lot of ailments. The doctor said he had heard the same story about broccoli, but he had no medical knowledge that broccoli can prevent ailments. He added that it contained a lot of beneficial nutrients.

The caller said; "But it's such an expensive vegetable to buy in the supermarket!"

The doctor said; "Do you have a greenhouse?"

The caller said; "No, I live in an apartment without a garden."

The doctor said; "then maybe you should arrange with family and friends to build a greenhouse and try planting vegetables like broccoli and strawberries". "These are not really tropical vegetables but you might grow them successfully in a greenhouse, and I don't mean the glass-type greenhouses. I meant the little wooden shed; they are much cooler than glass greenhouses."

♣♣♣♣♣

Shortly after the program ended, Malc returned home he walked into the kitchen. Dorothy asked her husband if he was ready for lunch.

Malc said; "I had a few beers with Josh and Melvin over by the paradise café, and something to eat. Oh, I forgot to water the plants in the greenhouse."

"Funny you should mention the greenhouse," said Dorothy. "I was just listening to a medical program over the radio, and someone called in with a question about broccoli."

Malc said; "What has broccoli got to do with medical problems?"

"The caller said she had read in a magazine article that broccoli can prevent ailments."

"Really; that sound like nonsense to me."

"No, the doctor said broccoli has some good nutrients. Malc, I know you don't like too many vegetables, but now we are older we need to change our diet. We should eat less of carbohydrates and add more salads and fresh fruits to our diet."

Malc said; "salad is grass you know, I'm a meat eater!" He continued; "well, anyway, I usually water the plants first thing in the morning, but it slipped my mind."

He stood up to go and water the plants in the greenhouse down the back garden.

Dorothy said; "why don't you leave it until this evening?"

"No, let me go and check; if they look wilted, then I will water them now."

He went and checked the plants in the shed at the bottom of the garden. He returned after fifteen minutes and told Dorothy the strawberries plants look wilted, so he gave them a little water, but the other plants looked okay.

Malc said; "The sun is very hot today, it sapped my energy; poor Gideon and them working on the building site."

Dorothy said; "That's why he always insists on wearing cotton clothes. He says they make him cooler but the hard hat gets very uncomfortable in this heat. Maybe that's why his hair is receding already."

Malc said; "No, I remember Josh's hair went like that when he was in his twenties; that type of soft hair would always go thin quickly."

"I suppose so, and when he gets hot, the salty sweat wouldn't help either."

"Anyway, I'm going to take a nap; you want to come?"

"Mr Melrose . . . you're still as frisky as ever."

"But darling . . . did I mention sex?"

"No, but that is what you implied when you invited me to the bedroom midday. You go and rest yourself; I need to work on the wedding dresses."

"Okay." He stood up from the chair and kissed his wife on the lips.

Chapter 5

Adam Melrose

Later that day, Adam arrived home and walked into the room where his mum was busy sewing the bridesmaid dresses. She stopped what she was doing and turned to her son.

"Mum, I have someone I would like you to meet; said Adam"

Adam was standing alone by the doorway, so Dorothy looked puzzled and asked, "Who is it, son?"

Adam turned towards the door and said, "Come in, Brenda."

Brenda walked in and Dorothy stood up.

"Mum, this is Brenda McKenny, my girlfriend."

"Hello, Mrs Melrose," said Brenda.

Dorothy stretched her right hand out and shook Brenda's hand. She said, "Hello, Brenda, pleased to meet you." She turned to her son and added, "So Adam, you finally own up to having a girlfriend."

Then she raised her arms and ushered Adam and Brenda to take a seat.

"It's a pity Adam's father isn't up; you should come again, Brenda, and meet the family properly. How about this Friday evening? I can cook something nice. Do you like tuna?"

Brenda said; "I like any kind of fish, well all the ones I've eaten so far. There isn't a fish that I don't like to eat."

Dorothy said; "Oh good . . ."

"By the way, I've already met Adam's sisters, and Annette has invited me to the wedding."

"Yes, I'm just making the bridesmaid dresses; well, I'm stitching two dresses, and Gideon's mum is doing the other two dresses. They should be ready by end of October, and then we have our own dresses to make. I'm wearing gold and Gideon's mum will wear a peach dress."

"Oh, that sounds like a nice colour co-ordination between the two mums."

"Brenda is your father the head master of the grammar school in Kingstown?"

"Yes, Mrs Melrose; do you know him?"

"I know your mum, Camilla; we went to Girls High School together, in the early fifties, long before your time. I used to be Dorothy Cunningham and your mum was Camilla Sanderson. We were in the same class; send my regards to her."

"I'm sure my mum would remember you if you were in the same class at high school."

Then Adam said; Mum this is just a quick hello as Brenda and I are meeting some friends to play a game of tennis. So she bid them goodbye and Brenda promise to come again to meet the rest of the family.

Dorothy went back to the sewing room and continued working while she listened to the radio. She was listening to a mix of her favourite soul and reggae music. She always thought it helped her to work better. Around three o'clock, Malc entered the room. By that time Paulina had left to fetch her children from school. Malc walked in the room where Dorothy was sewing the dresses.

He said; "I've slept for nearly two hours."

Dorothy said; "Yes, I've managed to finish quite a bit of sewing; the dresses are shaping up now."

Malc said; "That's good; I knew you would do a good job. I'll try not to look, leave it as a big surprise on the wedding day."

♣♣♣♣♣

A few hours later, the telephone rang; when Dorothy picked it up, she didn't recognise the caller's voice.

"Who is speaking?" asked Dorothy.

"Hello Dorothy, this is Camilla."

"Oh, hello, long time!"

Camilla said, "Yes I know; how are things? What a small world!"

Dorothy said, "Your daughter and my son got something going; who knows, we could even become family one day!"

Camilla said, "Yes, Adam is a lovely young man with good intentions."

Dorothy said, "It sounds like you know more than me . . ."

"No, no, I mean, you know young people these days show no manners. Well, your son is the complete opposite, he is so mannerly. Mike said the other day that he likes Adam because he is an ambitious young man. Mike never liked any of Brenda's friends, not even her girlfriends. Adam is the first one he has taken an interest in."

"That's good to hear," said Dorothy. "So do you have any more kids?"

Camilla answered, "Yes, I have another son who is younger than Brenda, his name is Brian, and he is at University in Barbados studying law. He wants to be a solicitor one day; he is nineteen and Brenda is twenty-one. What about yourself?"

"I started family life a few years before you. I have three children, two daughters older than Adam. Betsie, who is twenty-six, and Annette, twenty-four; she is getting married next June. Betsie is married Arnold Tilbury with a two-year-old son, Tony, so I'm a grandmother."

Camilla said, "So where is the wedding?"

"It's not too far from here it will take place at Bluemount Methodist Church."

"Oh yes, I know Rev. Monsolo, he is a nice man. We normally go to the Stream of Power Pentecostal Church. Our services are televised every Sunday."

"Yes, I know, I watch it sometimes."

"We'll have to meet up one day . . ."

"Yes, that would be nice."

Camilla said, "I have some friends coming for Bible lessons discussion. There is someone at the door, so I'll say bye for now, but we'll be in touch again soon."

"Okay, bye for now; and please say hello to your husband."

Dorothy didn't even place the phone back on the receiver; she just pressed the buttoned and dialled another number.

She rang Wilma; she counted six rings before Wilma answered.

Dorothy said, "Wilma . . . it's me; guess what?"

Wilma said, "What?"

"Do you remember Camilla Sanderson?"

"She went to Girls High?"

"Yes, the very lady. Adam introduced me to his girlfriend earlier today. His girlfriend's name is Brenda McKenny, and she is Camilla's daughter.

"What a small world we live in. I have not seen Camilla since we left high school, even though St Vincent is such a small place."

"Camilla is married to the head master of Boys Grammar School."

"Oh yes, I know Mr McKenny. The family goes to Streams of Power Church. She might want you to join them."

"I'm quite happy at Paradise Methodist, thank you. Anyway, we planned to meet up."

"Oh that's nice . . . can I come?"

"Of course you can come. We have a lot of catching up to do; in fact, twenty odd years would take a whole day."

"All right, just keep me posted."

Dorothy said, "Okay, bye."

Later on Dorothy told Malcolm he had missed the chance to meet Adam's girlfriend.

Malc said, "She must be special for him to bring her home to meet us."

"Yes, and guess who she is?"

"Go on tell me . . . someone we know?"

"Yes, she is the daughter of the head master of Boys Grammar School."

Malc said, "What, you mean Mr McKenny?"

"Yes and her mother Camilla and I used to go to Girls High School."

"Well I'll be damned," and then he sat down besides Dorothy at the dining table. "We should meet the McKenny family."

"I've already spoken to Camilla this morning.

"You don't waste time . . ."

Dorothy said, "She rang after I met her daughter, Brenda. Her mother was saying how much her husband liked Adam, and that he is a very nice young man, a credit to us. I agree, we've brought them up well, and we are lucky all three are doing nicely."

Malc put an arm around Dorothy and kissed her cheek. He said; two beautiful parents with three gorgeous children, and Dorothy replied; and now we have one grandchild. Malc said; and hopefully more to follow in the near future.

♣♣♣♣♣

As planned, that Friday evening Brenda arrived to meet Adam's parents and siblings for dinner at the family home. With all the family seated at the dining table, Brenda was certainly the centre of attention, as the conversation was mainly with her.

"Brenda, how long have you known my son; asked Adam's Dad?"

Brenda replied, "I went to Girls' High School next door from Adam's School, so I used to see him during lunch time."

Adam interrupted, "Yes, I used to look at her and thought she was my Miss World. But I was too shy five years ago to even say hello to her."

Brenda said, "Five years ago?"

"Yes," answered Adam.

Brenda said, "But I didn't even know you five years ago!"

Adam's Dad said, "Ah there you go . . . my son had romance on his mind from the first time he saw you!"

Everyone laughed, and then Adam's Mum said, "You two are still very young, so take time to get to know each other."

"Don't worry, Adam and I are not planning on getting married just yet; said Brenda."

Adam said, "Agreed; I want to get myself established as a TV producer."

Adam's Dad said, "That is an up and coming career to be in at the moment. St Vincent is taking off with some good TV soaps, plays, and movies."

Brenda was is a trainee midwife, and she told the family that one day she would like to run her own clinic of midwife nurses and infant aftercare workers.

Adam's Mum said, "We desperately need more nurses in that profession, so that would be an excellent career path for you Brenda."

Annette said, "How many babies have you delivered?"

"I have delivered three babies and was supcrvised by a matron. I have to follow this procedure with another senior midwife nurse for a twelve months period until I'm fully trained. Then I would have passed through my probation period. I absolutely love my job, and so far the three babies I delivered had no complications.

"Some babies can be in a breached position, which means the baby will not deliver safely. It could cause distress and danger, so I hope to encounter that type of problem now during my practise stages. I don't want to experience these problems later on when I'm working alone. Some mothers prefer to have their babies at home and that could be a bit risky."

Adam's Mum said, "The more babies you deliver, the more confident you become; it's a job you love doing, so you would be fine it's a good profession." Then eventually you could run your own clinic. That is my main ambition; said Brenda.

After dinner Adam's Mum said; Brenda, would you like to see some of our family photos? Adam said; "Oh no Mum, not that one of me sitting naked in the yellow plastic bath tub? So what's wrong with that; I'm sure by now Brenda has seen it . . . remarked Annette.

Later that evening Adam drove Brenda back home. She told Adam she felt so relaxed it was as if she knew the family years ago. My Dad is a cool dude; said Adam. Mum she is the best but I'm bias; I love all my family and I'm happy to say I'm very blessed, I could not ask for a better bunch of family. Brenda said; we must organise a party to meet my family and your family; my Mum had promised to ring your Mum again.

♣♣♣♣♣

Annette was up early at nine o'clock, unusual for her, as she normally tried to catch up on extra sleep at the weekends. But there was so much noise of traffic, car horns, and children shouting that morning, she couldn't have slept anyway. She swung open her bedroom window overlooking the main road and could see it was already a brilliant sunny morning. Immediately, she thought, *Today looks like it's going to be a picnic day on the beach.*

She rang her sister Betsie and asked her if she fancied going to the beach.

Betsie replied, "That's a good idea, I wonder if Brenda would like to come along."

Annette said, "Adam is still here, let me ask him. Oh, before I go, shall I roast a couple of breadfruits to bring for our lunch?"

"Yes and I could do some salt fish stew to go with it," replied Betsie.

"Okay, I'll see you at one-thirty; shall we go to Portvilla Beach or Colberry Beach?"

Annette said, "We'll come to Colberry, Portvilla Beach might be too crowded."

"Okay, see you shortly."

After Annette hung up the phone, she went straight to Adam's bedroom and saw he was still fast asleep; she decided not to disturb him, as it was still early.

Annette went to the kitchen and poured some water into the small milk pot, as she fancied some herbal tea and a couple of boiled eggs. She checked the tea cupboard and noticed some dried fever grass leaves her dad had brought back when they visited the farmland. She added a few dried leaves into the boiled water and allowed it to simmer. Ten minutes later, she strained the water into a mug and added sugar to taste. After breakfast, Annette showered and got dressed; it was still only eleven o'clock. She decided to allow Adam to sleep for at least another hour.

Just after noon, Adam was up; Annette heard him walking around in the bathroom. She shouted from downstairs, "Hey bruv, do you fancy going to the beach? I'm meeting Betsie, and you could bring Brenda."

"Where exactly are you planning to go . . . not Portvilla?" replied Adam. "I think Elson and his group are playing football there today."

"No, we are going to Colberry beach."

"Okay, can I ask Everton and Monica?"

"Yes, not too many of your friends though; I'm only roasting two breadfruits, and I'm baking some cupcakes."

"We could take some breadnuts and roast them on the beach too."

"Oh, let's take the coal pot and some other vegetables; Dad brought back a lot of tanias and plantains from the country. Some of those would do nicely."

"Sounds like a real barbecue to me."

Adam rang Brenda; she answered the phone after three rings and he said, "Hi babe."

"Hello, good looking," replied Brenda.

"Listen, my sisters are going to the beach. Wan come?"

"Yes, what time are you going?"

"I'll pick you up about at quarter to two."

"Okay, see you then."

Brenda went straight to put on her bathing suit and decided to wear one of her beach dresses. She chose a long red halter neck nylon dress and red rubber sandals; she pulled her hair back with a pony comb and put a little sun cream on her face, shoulders, and neck, and she added plenty of Vaseline on her lips.

She went to the fridge and wondered what drinks she should carry; she was going to pick some beers but then she thought, *Adam is driving, better not tempt him.* So she chose juicy beverages instead; she picked grape and banana flavours.

At precisely ten to two Adam pulled up by the front yard; there was Annette, Everton, Monica, and just enough space to squeeze Brenda in the car. Annette was sitting in the front seat next to her brother, so she got out and told Brenda she should sit next to her man.

They arrived at Colberry less than an hour later; Betsie was already at the beach with her son Tony, waving frantically. Betsie's neighbour Sallyanne was also with them; she had her son Ryan, who was the same age as Tony. The boys were good playmates; they made sand castles on the beach with their spades and plastic buckets.

Adam and Everton unloaded the picnic luggage, and Annette lit the coal pot fire to prepare some more barbeque food. Adam even carried a fold-up table, which was handy to put the drinks on. The roasted breadfruits Annette had prepared were already sliced and covered in foil. Betsie also prepared fish stew; she brought it in a big flask to keep it warm.

After stripping off into their swimwear, the two mums sat together with Tony and Ryan, making sand castles. Annette and Brenda listened to the music and began dancing to one of their favourite tunes by Bob Marley: "Could You Be Loved." Adam and Everton sat on the beach, admiring the two ladies dancing.

Adam said, "This is one of my favourite Bob Marley songs; the more I hear it, the more I like it!"

They decided to have lunch straight away. Betsie said, "Later on we could have the other roasted food."

Annette put some breadnuts in the hot coal pot vent, and within minutes they were popping and exploded.

So, to avoid more breadnut explosions, Betsie told Annette to make sure the breadnuts were well covered with the hot ash. They all sat in a group, enjoying the picnic lunch while they listened to the radio.

After lunch, Betsie, Annette, and Sallyanne took the two toddlers for a quick dip in the crystal clear sea water. Adam and Brenda found a hideaway on the beach and walked out of sight, as did Everton and Monica.

Betsie said, "We won't see those lovebirds until we are ready to leave."

Half an hour later, Annette remembered the roasting vegetables. She ran towards the coal pot and noticed that most of the food and drinks they'd left on the table had disappeared.

She shouted to Betsie and Sallyanne, "Hey, what happen to the food we left on the table?"

The ladies ran towards Annette with the boys following behind.

As they tried to figure out the missing food, Sallyanne said, "Well, I see the lovebirds didn't come back; so they are not our suspects."

Annette said, "Hey, look behind you over there, those kids are waving."

"It was them; they look guilty, and brazen with it too," said Betsie.

Betsie remembered the food roasting in the coal pot hot vent; she checked the tanias; these were just right, but the plantains were a bit burnt.

Sallyanne said, "Oh just give them a scrape; they'll still be edible."

"What about the breadnuts?"

Annette checked the hot vent and pulled out the foil; they were perfect.

Betsie said, "I still have some bottled water and juice in an ice box container. Thank God, I didn't put those out; the robbers would have helped themselves to everything."

Later on, the lovebird couples showed up. The first thing Adam noticed was that the drinks were missing from the table, because he was very thirsty by then, but before Adam could utter a word, the ladies said, "We were robbed."

Brenda replied, "By whom?"

Annette pointed towards the far end of the beach, where six teenage boys were playing football.

"Ah well, the thieving ragamuffins; no harm done, we still have the food we roasted."

They all sat down and ate some roasted vegetables with a bottle of juicy beverage each. Then around half an hour later, they gathered everything and loaded them in the car. The coal pot was still very hot, so Everton poured sea water on the burning coals. They waited fifteen minutes for the coal pot to cool down before loading it in the car boot.

On their way home, the sun was still shining brightly. The scenery as they drove through Colberry was breathtaking; the sea looked calm, like a big blue turquoise carpet. As Annette looked across the villages with admiration, she could see down in the valley, where there were many lovely homes.

Chapter 6

Adam's Play:
"Stay Away from Boys"

Adam's family sat in the living room to watch his first televised play, which he had filmed with some friends. Before he pressed play on the video machine, he explained the contents of the play to his family.

Adam said, "Mum and Dad, you may find some of the scenes a bit vulgar, but we've tried to make it as realistic as it can be."

Dad said, "Son, we know how young people behave nowadays. When your mum and I were teenagers, I'm happy to say we were much more innocent, and we enjoyed our childhood. But nowadays, TV and the Internet spoil it all. Go ahead, we will watch it, but I don't think we will be too surprised."

Betsie's son Tony was fast asleep in her arms; she went upstairs to put him down to sleep in the small bedroom. When she closed the door, she whispered, "Thank God you're asleep. No way would I sit and watch Adam's coarse play while you're awake." She returned downstairs in time to watch the start of the play.

Here is a synopsis of the play:

Jackie was still at school; her mom, Sandra, was bringing up Jackie singlehandedly. Sandra had Jackie when she was just fifteen; the father was a married man. When Jackie turned thirteen, Sandra began to warn her to stay out of trouble, saying that she must work hard in school. Sandra knew she could have a better future if she kept away from boys too. But Sandra never really explained to her daughter why she needed to stay away from boys.

The show commenced with a rendition of the Beatles' "All You Need Is Love." Jackie was now fourteen and involved with two men, one was eighteen years old, and the other was a forty-year-old married man.

One day, Jackie was walking home from school. A car pulled up, and it was Mr Moon, who worked for the town's Public Health Department (PHD). Jackie had met him when she accompanied her mum to the PHD in town. He opened the car door and offered her a lift home.

The next time Jackie saw him he offer her a lift and she sat down in the front seat. Mr Moon said, "You are such a beautiful young lady. I have something for you." He reached into the glove compartment and handed Jackie a shining new watch.

Jackie always wanted a watch, ever since she had learned in school how to tell the time, but her mother couldn't afford one. So she didn't hesitate to take the watch from Mr Moon, but he made her promise she would never allow her mum to see her wearing it, as it would raise suspicion. Later that evening, Jackie went next door to her best friend Cleo Gulip's house; she couldn't wait to show her the watch.

Jackie stretched her hand out, and Cleo remarked, "Wow, what a lovely watch; who bought it for you? I know it's not your birthday or anything."

"Oh, Mr Moon gave it to me," she said.

"What? Jackie, you need to be careful," Cleo said. "My mammy told me that some men are perverts. They tantalise you with gifts and woo you with their charms, then your mind plays tricks with your heart; you think you are in love . . . infatuation!

"Then comes the kiss, and when you kiss a man, you become addicted to his charms. Before you know it, you will be sneaking out from home to meet up with Mr Moon. For goodness sake; he is a married man. There's a reason I'm telling you this: when my mammy was sixteen, her mother died and she went to live with her aunty, who had a son and daughter about the same age. One day she was at home alone when a neighbour an adult family friend came over. He forced himself onto her and raped her, but instead of resenting him, she fell head over heels in love with him. She carried on entertaining him with their guilty pleasures.

"So take this as a warning; in the adult world we need to recognise real love; when love is real, there is no doubt in your mind. It is a special bond between two people. And the way to know the difference; is true love makes you feel happy, safe, and secure . . . without a single doubt. By all means, Jackie, you should keep the gift, but don't succumb to Mr Moon's bait; don't kiss him! Stay away from that dirty married man."

As Jackie listened to Cleo, she knew it was too late, as she had already kissed Mr Moon. He had told her not to tell anyone, as it was a secret between them.

Two months later, as she walked home from school, she met Colin, who was just a few years older than her. He started touching her face, and the next thing she knew, he was kissing her lips. It felt good, like she felt when Mr Moon had kissed her.

Jackie wondered if this was why Mammy kept telling her that she should stay away from boys. Then she pushed Colin away and ran as fast as she could to the busy main road. She saw a car coming towards her; as it got closer, she realised it was Mr Moon.

He stopped and opened the door besides him and said, "Where you going in such a hurry?" He noticed she was shaking and asked, "You all right, baby?"

Then she got in the car and sat down next to Mr Moon.

"What's the matter, baby?" he asked. "I don't like to see you sad. Tell me . . ."

He stretched his arm around Jackie and pulled her closer. Before she could speak, he began kissing her passionately.

Jackie remembered how it felt the first time he kissed her. Mr Moon could do anything to her, she thought. He started to reach for her breast, and it felt even better. Then he began to stroke her thighs, and she felt a deep sensation.

Mr Moon whispered, "You are so heavenly," and Jackie thought; *don't stop!*

He stopped suddenly and said, "Can I meet you later?"

Jackie remembered her mum had warned her to stay away from boys. But Mr Moon was a grown man; she started to answer but Mr Moon put his finger on Jackie's lips. He told her it would be okay. "Just tell your mum you are meeting your friends to go over some homework; we won't be out late," he said.

Jackie said, "Okay, see you later," and she left his car.

First Island Cover Girl

Sandra had made a big mistake: she had warned Jackie to stay away from boys but failed to explicitly explain the consequences of sexual intercourse.

Adam's dad spoke first; Malc said, "Son, that is an amazing show that everyone can relate to . . . it might even stir up some lively debates."

♣♣♣♣♣

About six months later, Adam had filmed part two of the play. His family had given him some helpful critiques of his first episode play, and he valued their honesty. One night, all the family gathered at his parents' home to watch part two.

Jackie knocked on the door of Cleo's home; she prayed that it would be Cleo who would answer the door. Jackie was waiting with her fingers crossed behind her back; "Please God; let it be Cleo, not Mrs Gulip."

Her prayers were answered; Cleo opened the door, and when she set eyes on her friend, it was obvious Jackie was very upset. "Lord, have mercy!" "Are you okay?" Cleo asked. "What's the matter with you? You look like you seen a ghost!"

Jackie tried to stay calm but couldn't, as tears flowed down her face. Cleo pulled Jackie inside and said, "Shh . . ."

Before Cleo's mum noticed, the two girls rushed to the bedroom. They both sat on the bed, but Jackie stood up again quickly as if she sat on spikes; then Jackie asked Cleo for a panty pad.

Cleo said, "Oh, an emergency? Is that why you look so upset? You've got your period it caught you unaware and you are not wearing a pad?"

Jackie said, "No, no, no . . ."

Cleo said, "Well, what then?"

Jackie said, "I'm bleeding but it's not my period . . ."

Cleo said, "Oh my God . . . what then?"

Jackie said, "Mr Moon . . . took my virginity!"

"He forced himself on you?" remarked Cleo. "Oh my good Lord, he raped you? Let me tell Mammy; she will know what to do."

Jackie said, "No, no, please don't . . ."

Cleo stood up from her bed and said, "Are you crazy? You have to tell your mum or the police! This is a married man! I warned you; men like him are just old perverts."

Then Cleo said, "Oh my God! You could be pregnant!"

Jackie said, "What do you mean?"

Cleo said, "Girl, when you have intercourse, you could get pregnant, I thought you knew that Jackie?"

Jackie cried and cried until she fell asleep on the floor in Cleo's bedroom.

Cleo didn't disturb her but told her mum that Jackie had fallen asleep in her bedroom. Her dad said not to wake her up; he would call round at her mother and tell her that Jackie was staying over.

Cleo covered her friend with a blanket and left her undisturbed asleep on the floor.

Jackie slept right through until next morning. Around six o'clock, she opened her eyes and wondered where she was. She realised she was with Cleo and then remembered the disaster from the night before.

Jackie said aloud, "Oh God, what a mess I'm in!"

Cleo was awakened by Jackie's voice.

She sat up in her bed and whispered to her friend, "I still think you should tell someone; this is too big a secret for us to keep to ourselves."

Jackie said, "No, I can't tell anyone. I can't take the shame."

Cleo remarked, "It will be even more shameful if you really are pregnant!"

Jackie missed her period and began to realise that she was pregnant. She thought, *this is too much for me to go on, and I must do something to end this pain and humiliation.*

The following Saturday morning, she helped her mother wash some laundry and noticed the bottle of bleach. Jackie's mind was working overtime with negative thoughts. She thought, *maybe if I drink some of the bleach that would end my pain.* Jackie didn't think for a moment that bleach would poison her, even end her life.

That night, Jackie went to the cupboard, held her nose, and drank some of the bleach. She went to her room and lay down; the next morning, Jackie's mother couldn't wake her up.

Sandra screamed as she tried to wake her daughter. She kept shouting, "Jackie, Jackie! Wake up!" She tried for half an hour to no avail. Sandra realised her daughter was dead; she ran as fast as she could to Cleo's home. Sandra shouted, "Jackie is dead; she is not moving!"

By then Mrs Gulip ran from the kitchen and into the front yard; she held onto Sandra. "What do you mean, Jackie is dead?" Mrs Gulip said.

"We saw her yesterday . . . she looked a bit sad but I thought that's down to being a teenager."

Cleo couldn't keep the secret any longer; she said, "Jackie was pregnant!"

Mrs Gulip replied, "What? Well, maybe she had complications."

By then Cleo had her hands on her head and tears were flowing steadily; she said; "No, no, she was raped!"

Sandra screamed aloud; "Who raped her?"

"Mr Moon raped her!"

Mrs Gulip and Sandra looked at each other. Cleo's mother said; "Child, what you talking 'bout?"

"Mr Moon raped her!" repeated Cleo.

Sandra said; "You mean that nice man who works for the Public Health Department in town?"

Cleo said; "Yes, I warned her not to go."

Sandra said; "Go where?"

Cleo said; "She went to see him three months ago."

Mrs Gulip said; "You mean that night when she stayed at our house?"

Sandra said, "Lord Jesus, let me go to see the police right now! Jackie . . . deaddddddd! Oh!"

Mrs Gulip said; "I will come with you."

About twenty minutes later, they arrived at the police station.

Sandra said, "Officer, please help me. Me daughter deadddddddd . . ."

The Officer raised his arms and said, "Please, please, calm down! I am Officer Jones; please tell me your name."

"I am Sandra Conker," she said.

"Now what can I do for you?"

Sandra said, "Officer Jones, this morning I noticed Jackie wasn't up; she is the first one up every morning. So I went to her bedroom and tried to wake her and she didn't move . . . Jackie is dead!"

Sandra looked at her neighbour; she couldn't continue.

Mrs Gulip said, "Officer Jones, my name is Mrs Gulip, and this is my daughter Cleo. Cleo was Jackie's best friend." She turned to her daughter and said, "Tell the officer what you know . . ."

Cleo said, "Well, three months ago, Jackie came to our house, and she was very upset, crying and bleeding, but it wasn't her period; she said Mr Moon raped her."

Sandra became outraged; raising her arms high, she cried, "My daughter is only fifteen years old."

The officer said; "I thought you said she was dead . . ."

"She is; she *was* only fifteen years old!"

Officer Jones said; "Do you realise this is serious allegation? For a start, if this happened three months ago, why didn't you come here before now?"

Sandra said; "This is news to me; I didn't realise my young daughter was pregnant; she was only fifteen years old!"

Officer Jones said; "We can carry out a post-mortem on your daughter to ascertain whether she was pregnant and then take it from there. In the meantime, I will send a detective to your home to investigate—this is now a crime scene."

The autopsy concluded that Jackie was pregnant. They questioned Mr Moon, but he denied raping Jackie, saying he had never been in contact with the young girl. Mr Moon was released without charge.

The play ended with this quote:

"It takes just one mistake to rein your whole life . . ."

Chapter 7

Christmas

Josh LeBoun often felt concerned about the amount of electricity people used around Christmas time. Wilma would remind her husband that he was too grumpy every time he complained. She would say to him, "Stop thinking about electricity bill. What about our grandchild? Think how lovely the Christmas decorations would excite him!"

Then Josh would give a long speech about how things were when he was growing up. He said, "We used to make do with a balloon as our Christmas gift. If we were lucky we would get a flute, you know the paper flute that you blow out and it curls back in."

Wilma said, "Yes, they still sell them, but kids today; toys for them are normally computerised gadgets."

Josh smiled and said; "and they are very expensive too!" A computer is good and it's bad; kids don't get enough exercise because they sit using a computer instead of running about in the yard. In my days, we were more resourceful and used our imaginations for certain; we were more adventurous!

Wilma replied, "Yes, that is true, and it was safer for us."

Josh said, "How you mean safer?"

"The computer is not safe for kids . . . they are exposed to criminals too, you know!

But Adam said you can control and monitor what kids do on the Internet. By the way, what are we buying Danny for his Christmas?"

Josh said, "I was looking at a tricycle in the shop."

Wilma said, "He would love something like that; we should mention this to his parents. I've already bought him some books."

Josh said, "What about crayons and colouring books?"

Wilma said, "That too! I wished we didn't give away the *Little Red Riding Hood* and the *Three Little Pigs story* books."

Josh said, "Do you remember how the children used to enjoy listening to us reading to them? James used to ask me to read the *Three Little Pigs* over and over again, until me wise up and recorded the story on cassette tape. *It worked a treat as he used to settle down in bed and listened to the tape until he fell asleep.* "

Later on in the evening, the family went to a Christmas show held at the Abbey Vale playing field. There were lots of Christmas decorations, reindeers, various lights, and people dressed as Santa Claus. There was a nativity set all made of wood by a local carpenter, including two little sheep covered in real wool. Gideon thought it was very clever and asked who created them. A lady told him it was done by a young autistic man.

Gideon was impressed by the intricately designed work of art and went to see the inventor. His name was Des Tantan; he was nineteen years old and lived with his mother, she raised him singlehandedly. Irena Tantan was forty and made baskets and sold vegetables from her garden to the neighbours to earn a living. She always gave her son undivided attention and treated him as if he was full-bodied and alert; never one day did she think of her son as slow.

Gideon was very impressed by the work he had seen; he thought Des Tantan was a genius. So he introduced himself to Irena, saying, "Hello, my name is Gideon LeBoun."

Irena said, "Yes, I know you—you are the builder. You're building up some lovely houses in the neighbourhood, man. That house at Portvilla is beautiful . . . I'd never be able to afford a house like that, though."

Gideon said, "Never say never; anything is possible. Ms Tantan, does your son have a job?"

Irena said, "Job? Nobody wants to employ him. You see, only a few people understand autistic people; yes, they are difficult, but it takes patience and understanding. My son is very capable, and his gift is to create things. Mr LeBoun, you just need to show him something once, and he can make a replica model of it."

Gideon said, "I think I can employ your son. I need someone to mould wood into shapes for my property work."

Irena said, "True? You think you could give him a steady job?"

Gideon said, "Yes, of course."

Irena called her son over from where he was standing and introduced him to Gideon.

Gideon said, "How would you like to come and work with me, Des? I'm in the building trade, I build houses. I think you could come and work for me making models. Do you want to see the type of designs I have in mind?"

Des said, "Yes, okay!"

"I'll be right back," and then he walked over to his truck. He came back carrying a folder with a list of gable decorations.

Des turned the pages through the catalogue and said, "Yes, I can make all of those."

Irena said, "This is work he could do from home; he already has a work shop set up in our garden shed."

Gideon said, "That sounds perfect; can I drop by tomorrow?"

The next day Gideon went to see Des as promised; he was amazed to see the amount of work Des had done. Some of his wood carvings were so good, he purchased them right there. Then Gideon showed him the designs he wanted Des to make up for him. Des told him what type of wood he needed, and they agreed on cost and salary. Gideon wanted Des to start work straightaway, and they both shook hands on the deal.

Chapter 8

Wedding

By end of January, Dorothy and Wilma had completed the wedding outfits. On the Saturday, they arranged for the bridal party to meet at Dorothy's home for a final fitting of the wedding outfits.

Malc and Josh thought they were making a lot of fuss, since they insisted that no one else be present.

Malc said, "What's the big secret anyway?"

Dorothy said, "It would make a lovely surprise on the wedding day to see the bridal party's dresses for the first time."

The moment came for the catwalk to begin, and Wilma and Dorothy were very proud of their achievements. Everyone thought the dresses looked perfect.

Wilma said, "Annette, you picked the right colours that compliment our skin tone."

The ladies were standing in front of a big mirror. Dorothy said, "The gold suits me because I'm darker than Wilma. And Wilma, the peach suits your skin shade perfectly." Dorothy turned to admire Wilma; she added, "Cream shoes would match with your peach or even black if you prefer." I think the cream shoes will do perfectly; replied Wilma.

♣♣♣♣♣

The Wedding

Five months had passed, and only two weeks to go before the big day. As scheduled, the bridal group went to the church for rehearsal. Annette and Gideon were shown the wedding leaflets, and they were content that the agenda was all in place, hymns, and Bible readings. Annette and Gideon read through the wedding leaflets, and happy with the end product thought they looked very professional and well designed.

Rev. Monsolo led the bride and groom through the ceremony's step-by-step process. Then it was the bridal party's turn bridesmaids, and parents, of both bride and groom acted out their part in the procession.

♣♣♣♣♣

A day before the wedding, the caterers gathered at Wilma's house and prepared the meals and packed them away in plastic containers in the fridge. For last minute preparations, Dorothy and Wilma's assistants planned to meet Saturday morning to prepare the salads. The men all gathered at Gideon's new home on Friday night, where they planned to get ready next day.

On Saturday morning, Annette's alarm clock went off at six a.m. She opened her eyes and realised the big day had arrived. The wedding day that seemed like a long wait for Annette was finally here on a bright sunny morning. She sat up in bed and kept repeating, "Mrs Annette LeBoun, the wife of Gideon LeBoun. Then she thought one day, we will have four children. Annette thought quietly; I would love to be blessed with two girls and two boys. My daughters' names will be Mari and Rosanna; oh, the surname goes well together."

As she drifted back from her sub-conscious mind, she got out of bed and stretched her arms as far as they would go. The phone rang and straight away she knew it was Gideon. She picked up the receiver.

Gideon said; "Hi Hon; are you ready to become my wife?"

"Of course I'm ready."

"Not as much as I'm ready to be your husband! I am excited and ready for our honeymoon to Jamaica, where our first born will be conceived."

"What are you saying, Mr LeBoun? You're not wasting time then; shouldn't we wait a few months?"

"Mrs LeBoun, you and I agreed we are going to have a big family. Anyway, I'll let you go and turn yourself into my beautiful princess. See you later, sweetheart . . . kisses."

Annette went to the kitchen and prepared herself a big breakfast, as she needed to start the day full of energy. After breakfast she thought, *it wouldn't matter now if I don't have anything to eat all day.* Annette left her family to eat breakfast in the kitchen; she went to the lounge and checked the wedding leaflet again. It made her nervous, and for the first time she realised it was going to be a nerve racking day. All the attention was going to be on her. Annette thought; *I can't wait for the party to begin*, as she knew that she wouldn't be able to relax until after the wedding ceremony.

Annette called her best friend Eloise; for certain she could calm her down with some funny jokes. Annette explained to Eloise how nervous she felt. Eloise said, "I can fix that; listen to this joke."

Eloise said, "One day this woman was walking over a bridge, and it was very windy. Her dress blew right up over her head, but instead of trying to keep her dress down; she held onto her head.

A young man was walking by, and he said; 'Lady, your dress is blowing up and all you could do is hold onto your head?'

The lady replied, 'Son, down below is eighty years old; I don't have anything to offer no man. I'm hanging onto my head because it's a new wig!'

Annette couldn't stop laughing, but when she caught her breath, she said to Eloise, "Thank you; darling, see you later!"

Annette thought the morning had passed slowly. At around noon, eager for the most nerve racking hour to pass. The bridal party were all gathered at her parents' house; the hairdresser came to style her hair and make-up. After her hair and make-up were done, she was almost ready. She just needed to freshen up and get dressed. Betsie was first to finish getting dressed, followed by the bridesmaids and her mum, and then it was Annette's turn.

With the bridal group ready, Betsie helped her sister into her bridal gown. She looked absolutely stunning; her dress had enough sequins to light up a dark bedroom. As soon as Dorothy saw her daughter, tears welled up in her eyes.

Annette said; "Mum, I don't want you to start me off crying!"

When Annette's Mum saw her daughter, she said; "You look as radiant as when Betsie got married to Arnold three years ago."

Betsie said, "I remember my wedding day as if it was yesterday, and I'm still very much in love with Arnold. Sis, it's going to be a fabulous day today, don't be nervous; as soon as you walk into the church and you set eyes on Gideon, you will feel calm."

At mid-day two wedding cars pulled up outside the Melrose front yard. Malc came out of the first car and walked into the lounge, where the bridesmaids were waiting. He was amazed and didn't speak for a few seconds. "You all look stunning," he finally said.

Then Dorothy walked in.

Malc said; "Wow, Mrs Melrose, you look as radiant as the day I married you!"

Dorothy said; "Thank you Hon, and you look as handsome as the day I met you!"

Then his two glamorous daughters appeared, Annette dressed in her sparkly white dress and a long veil trailing behind her. Betsie, wearing a maxi powder blue dress, was right behind her.

"You all look heavenly," said their proud dad. He turned to Dorothy and said, "Darling, those dresses are beautiful; you've done a fabulous job."

A few minutes later, Dorothy and the bridesmaids left in the first bridal car. Annette and her Dad followed in the second bridal car.

The proud Dad helped his daughter out of the car in the church yard, and they could hear the Elvis Presley song playing, "It's Now; or Never," and then the music stopped. As Annette and her Dad walked up the aisle, "Here Comes the Bride" was played. The church was packed with families and friends the bridesmaids looked fashionable in powder blue outfits and both mothers in their gold and peach dresses looked stunning. And the men in gray suits, blue shirt, and tie that complimented the bridesmaids dress. An hour later the wedding service ended, and Gideon and Annette left church as husband and wife.

The wedding reception was held at the church hall. There was a huge flowers garden and green lawn the most perfect background scene for their wedding photos. There were yellow, red, white, and orange roses; pink and white hibiscus; and purple forget-me-nots trimmed the garden walkway. After the photos session ended, Annette felt much more relaxed at the reception. The best man did an excellent speech he was entertaining and everyone enjoyed his comical jokes.

Then it was the DJ's turn to get down to business; first he played Percy Sledge "Cover me," dedicated to the newlyweds. After that song the bride and groom's parents took turns to dance with the newlyweds. Annette danced with her father-in-law, and Gideon danced with his mother-in-law, Annette's Dad danced with Gideon's mother. The DJ played a mix of music, and all of the guests enjoyed the wedding party. They danced until the early hours of Sunday morning. But Annette and Gideon left before mid-night he had organised overnight stay at the Starlight Guest House for their first night as husband and wife. Gideon told his wife that when they return from honeymoon he had planned a small celebration at their new home. And he had arranged for Rev Monsolo to bless their new home witness by all the families. He hugged his wife, kissed her tenderly, and whispered, "Mrs LeBoun, this is the beginning of a new chapter."

The next morning at the Guest House, Gideon was up at eight o'clock, very late for him. He left his wife in bed fast asleep and went for a jog near to the Guest House down by the beach. An hour later after Gideon returned from jogging, Annette opened her eyes and he was sitting in the chair next to the bed smiling and gazing at her. She stretched her arms out wide, and almost like a magnet her husband stood up from the chair and fell into her arms embraced her.

Gideon said, "Sleep well, Hon?"

"Like a top; answered Annette"

He joked, "I know; you were snoring."

"I don't snore!"

Gideon said, "I was just joking, but if you did it, wouldn't matter . . . because I want to wake up with you every day for the rest of my life."

♣♣♣♣♣

Honeymoon in Jamaica

Gideon and Annette's honeymoon flight to Jamaica was at two o'clock, but before they left, the newlyweds went to thank their parents. All the families agreed it was a fabulous wedding day and wished them all the very best in Jamaica. Annette's Dad told them they would enjoy Negril Beach. "It's a beautiful place," he said. "Jamaica is a beautiful island."

"The beaches in Jamaica are lovely, better than the beaches in St Vincent," remarked her Mum.

At one o'clock, the Melrose and LeBoun families gathered at the airport to wave off Annette and Gideon on their flight to Jamaica. It was Annette and Gideon first trip to Jamaica. Gideon thought it would be like a home away from home because the Caribbean region has one culture, language, music, and food.

They landed in Jamaica at the Manley International Airport and a taxi took them to the hotel. They spent two weeks sightseeing, first stop they went to the falls at Dunn's River in Ocho Rios. They also took a trip to the famous Rose Hall Museum; as they stood outside the balcony at Rose Hall they thought the views from the hill top overlooking the sea and surrounding villages were spectacular. Annette made certain she took lots of photos. Gideon told her one day she would be able to show the photos to their children.

After two weeks had ended, Annette and Gideon returned to St Vincent. They couldn't believe how fast two weeks time had passed. But they were happy to have a most memorable time, and equally pleased to return home to their family. They arrived in St Vincent in the evening, and both parents were waiting to greet them at the Airport. They drove straight to their new home that Gideon had built in Paradise Village. All the families were gathered in the front yard grandparents, parents, siblings, and Rev Monsolo. Gideon and Annette walked from the car and stood next to the Rev.

Rev Monsolo spoke; "We are very happy that you have returned from your honeymoon safely". I could certainly see from your glowing faces that you've enjoyed your time in Jamaica. Your families and I are gathered here to mark the beginning of your married live and to bless your new home.

"May God bless you both as you begin your life together as Mr and Mrs LeBoun . . . all the families clapped and then they toasted the couple; "we wish you a long and happy life together". Annette's mum shouted; and to my grandchildren in the next future . . . .

The house had five bedrooms, three bathrooms, and two en-suite shower rooms; one of the en-suite shower rooms was attached to Gideon and Annette's bedroom. Annette went straight to her bedroom; someone had made the bed, and it was just as inviting as the luxury hotel room in Jamaica. There were several heart-shaped balloons floating around the bedroom. She thought it looked like something out of a movie.

Annette said, "Who decorated the room?"

"Annette's mum; your big sister did it, sweetheart; do you like it?"

By that time, Gideon had joined her in the bedroom; he opened his mouth wide in amazement and said, "Wow, love is in the air all around." He turned to Annette and said, "Can you feel it, Hon?"

"You bet I feel it, Hon!"

Gideon realised they couldn't stay in the bedroom with the family waiting downstairs. He put his arm around Annette and whispered, "Later; let's go downstairs to join the party."

The ladies sat in the kitchen as the men listened to music on the radio in the lounge. Annette walked into the kitchen with a big grin on her glowing face.

Dorothy spoke first; she said, "My darling, you look fabulous; we don't need to ask if you had a good time in Jamaica!"

Annette answered, "Yes, Mum, Jamaica was divine; plenty to eat, and their beaches are heavenly. I even loved the way they speak; they are quite comical even when they don't mean to be."

Betsie said; "So Sis, do you think you are pregnant yet?"

"I don't think so—but it's not from lack of trying."

Wilma said; "My son is a romantic like his dad!"

Dorothy replied; "The Melroses got it too, love."

The women laughed loudly.

Annette said; "*You know what? I miss Gideon.*" My goodness, Gideon is only next door, I know it must be the intense love Sis; said Betsie.

"I'm certain you got enough intense love to last you until tonight .... ha ha ha!"

The family stayed a short while and then left the lovebirds. Annette felt lucky she had dinner prepared for her. Firstly, they had lots of wedding gifts to open; after that, they could relax in their new home.

Annette opened a dinner set from her grandparents Claudius and Doreen Melrose; next was a set of heavy silver cutlery from Gideon's grandparents Jack and Wendy LeBoun. "We will invite them to dinner one Sunday very soon," said Gideon. Both grandparents lived up north; Gideon's grandparents lived in Bramby, and Annette's grandparents lived in Dorchester Village. Annette recalled spending August holidays with her grandparents; she often said it was the most adventurous times she could remember as a child.

After they'd opened all of the gifts, the lounge was filled with gift paper and boxes everywhere. Gideon said, "Oh, sit down, sweetheart, we can tidy later."

He was busy tuning the new TV; everything looked fuzzy. Annette said she didn't understand why TV didn't come already tuned and ready to use. Gideon said, "Ah, you would still fiddly with it even when it was already tuned; it won't take that long."

He was right; first she could see channel 1, then 2, and so on.

There were lots of channels from the cable TV; most shows were from America. Annette said, "They all look like the same kind of trash."

Gideon said, "I thought you have your favourite soap you tune into every day?"

"Yes, I suppose I'm addicted to some of the TV soaps. Thank God tomorrow is Sunday. I can relax before I go back to work on Monday morning. I will take some wedding cake for my colleagues."

Gideon said; "What? But they were all at the wedding."

"Yes, but you know some of my colleagues would say they didn't get any of the cake; besides, it's tradition to take some to work. There is still plenty leftover."

The two lovebirds settled down to watch TV; they sat together closely, two hearts almost beating as one. Half an hour later, Annette was fast asleep, followed by Gideon. Two hours later, when Annette opened her eyes, she said, "I needed that sleep; I felt exhausted we've had a long day."

They both stood up and went to the kitchen; Gideon had a beer and Annette made a hot drink of ovaltine.

The next day Sunday morning, Gideon and Annette went to church; Rev Monsolo gave a special thank you prayer for the newlyweds' safe return journey from their honeymoon. Annette enjoyed her first Sunday in the kitchen, cooking her husband's favourite Sunday meal.

Chapter 9

First Island Cover Girl—Mari LeBoun

Six months after Annette and Gideon's wedding day, they invited the family over for dinner. They were all seated at the dining table and Annette said; "Gideon and I have some good news . . ."

Annette's mum couldn't stop herself; she clapped her hands and, with a broad grin on her face, said, "Oh, are you pregnant?"

Annette smiled and said, "Mother, please let me speak; yes, we are expecting our first baby. I'm three months pregnant."

Gideon's dad was sitting opposite him at the dining table; he stood up, reached over, and patted his son on his shoulders, as if he had won a competition.

Josh said, "Well done, son!"

No one could stop smiling, and then they settled down to eat.

Betsie asked her sister, "Have you thought of names yet?"

Annette's mum said, "Don't choose any old names."

Everyone laughed.

"No, you are right; we will choose a modern name. We like the name Mari if it's a girl, but we are undecided about a boy's name, replied Annette."

Annette's dad said, "Plenty of time left to decide a boy's name."

♣♣♣♣♣

In the month of June, Annette went into labour; she chose to deliver her baby at Kingstown General Hospital rather than a home birth. On Tuesday morning, June 18, she delivered a baby girl. They named her Mari; the lovely baby girl had a full head of hair and weighed eight pounds. Gideon was present at the birth, and the next day he drove his wife and newborn baby daughter home. Gideon couldn't keep away from her crib; he kept holding her, and he must have kissed her hundreds of time during the first days.

When Annette fell asleep, Gideon felt obliged to sit all night and keep watch over his precious gift. "Mari LeBoun," he kept repeating, saying her name over and over again. Gideon fell asleep in the chair next to the baby's cradle. Annette slept for three hours, shortly after that Mari was awake and began to bawl. Gideon jumped up from the chair . . . as if startled by the noise.

He saw Annette reaching for Mari. She smiled and said, "Go to bed, honey, I'll guard her now . . . proud Dad!"

He kissed Annette and whispered, "I love you and baby Mari." Gideon climbed into bed and began to snore immediately.

The next morning, grandparents Melrose were their first visitors. Grandma Dorothy held her granddaughter for the first time, whilst granddad looked on affectionately. Grandma Dorothy thought of offering help to bathe her but then she thought, no, Annette should do it first, so she decided to supervise instead.

Gideon's parents were the only family members missing; they were recovering from a spell of flu, so they stayed away. The remaining LeBoun family visited later that day; great-grandparents arrived first, and Gideon's brothers Sam and James, and Laverne. All of the family adored baby Mari as soon as they set eyes on her. Laverne was overjoyed as she now had one of each nephew Danny, and niece Mari.

Mari was three months old when she got christened. Grandma Wilma made her christening gown, and Grandma Dorothy baked a lovely cake for the christening party. The christening gown was a long ivory taffeta material designed with cream lace; it was absolutely beautiful. At church that day Baby Mari was well behaved; and certainly, the centre of attraction.

After the christening service, the entire family gathered at Gideon and Annette's home. Mari's big day was enjoyed by all; she was passed from arm to arm. Her mother thought she wouldn't be able to settle her after the family had left. But she was wrong; Mari slept soundly that night.

Annette was pleasantly surprised at how supportive Gideon was; he always made sure he was home early to put Mari to bed. Sometimes he even danced with her if she was moody, it often helped Mari to settle and she fell asleep easily.

♣♣♣♣♣

Two years later, Annette and Gideon had a son, named Colin. When Mari turned five, she started school, and Annette became pregnant with their third child. Colin went to preschool, which was adjacent to the primary school Mari attended. This suited Annette, as she was still working part-time at the airport.

Annette's third child was due in May 1977. She went on maternity leave just four weeks before her baby was born. The day before Annette went on maternity leave, the airport lounge was fairly quiet. She noticed all her co-workers were gathering at her desk. The manager, Mr DeRose, was there, which was very rare, as he never left his office.

Annette's colleagues gathered around her desk and presented her with a huge bouquet of flowers. The vase was filled with a rainbow of tropical flowers—absolutely beautiful. Mr DeRose presented the bouquet to Annette and said, "I wish all the very best for you; hope you have a bouncing baby boy!"

Annette was relieved to put her feet up, even though she watched the clock to collect the other children from school. She was lucky their grandparents were very supportive, and thank God, they both lived quite close. And of course her husband continued to be very loving and supportive; Annette often said he was the best any woman could wish for.

Annette already had been through this when she was pregnant with Mari and Colin; her immediate thought was; *this is the third and last time.* She didn't want any more children. The second week in May, Annette went into labour and delivered another boy; they named him Marvin. Gideon was more than happy with two boys; he was a very proud dad, and Mari was the apple of his eye.

Chapter 10

Mari Entrance Exam

At the age of twelve Mari was near the end of primary school days, and first she had to sit secondary school entrance exam. When Mari woke up that morning, she realised it was secondary school entrance exam day. She opened her eyes wider and jumped out of her bed. Then she grabbed her bath towel and headed straight to the bathroom; after using the toilet she brushed her teeth. Mari always thanked God for her perfectly shaped white teeth. She had a quick shower, quick, because Mari normally took thirty minutes, but that morning she was in a rush and only scrubbed her body for ten minutes.

She dried herself quickly in her bedroom and then stood in front of her wardrobe, wondering what she should wear, but then she realised there wasn't much time for that. So she grabbed a short sleeve white blouse and a short denim skirt with the edges frayed and got dressed in no time. She put on her sky blue suede flat shoes that had a lovely silver bow. She pulled her hair back in a pony tail and quickly ran downstairs before her mum called her again.

She entered the kitchen. "Good morning, Mother," she said; she normally called her "Mum," but whenever Mari wanted to be extremely polite she used "Mother" instead. Mari loved coffee but that morning her mum made chocolate drink.

Annette said, "This will help you to concentrate, as coffee would make you too hyped up. You need all the memory you have to pass that entrance exam, and may the Lord help you today, child. I want all my children to have a good education."

"Yes Mum, but I'm going to be a supermodel."

Annette said, "You can be anything you want to be, but just in case that doesn't work out, you need something to fall back on. So take this opportunity to work hard and get some qualifications . . . today could be the beginning of that dream.

"When you have qualifications, they cannot be erased; you need to plan well for the future. You don't want to be in the same situation as me. I got married too young, but I was lucky. Your father is a wonderful man, always putting his family first. I would have loved to be a teacher." Annette works at the Airport checking desk; she absolutely hated that job but it was a way to earn money. It was always her ambition to be a teacher, but destiny led her to a different path.

Mari said to her mother, "It's not too late to be a teacher; you are only thirty-five years old. You could go back to training college."

By the time Mari finished breakfast it was nearly eight o'clock; the entrance exam commenced at nine. It was a twenty-minute drive to the school hall, and her father had promised to drive her. Gideon went out early to the building site, where he had twenty men working on some apartment buildings.

Mari rushed upstairs to get the bag she had packed the night before. She didn't need to take much, just a ruler and pens. She looked in the mirror and added a little vaseline on her lips. Mari heard her dad shouting, "Ready, Mari?"

She ran out and jumped into the front seat of the truck where her dad was waiting with the engine cranked up, raring to go.

He said, "Are you nervous, Mari?"

Mari said, "Of course not, Dad. I'm a bright girl; this exam should be easy for me, and anyway, it's just general knowledge, common sense questions."

Dad said, "Don't get too complacent even common sense questions could trick you; just stay focused and do your best. This school is one of the best in St Vincent; most of the teachers come from England and Canada."

Mari said, "Dad, are you saying that we don't have good local teachers in St Vincent?"

Dad said, "No darling, that's not what I'm saying, but I can't help thinking that the Canadian and English teachers speak the English language better than we do. We tend to use Creole dialect and mess up good English language. So this is the best chance you'll get to be taught by a person who is English."

On the way to the school, Mari saw her best friend, Asia. She lived close to the school, so Mari asked her dad to stop and give Asia a lift.

Asia climbed into the front seat next to Mari.

Asia said, "Good morning, Mr LeBoun."

Gideon said, "Hello Asia, how are you today? Are you ready for your exam?"

Asia said, "I'm a bit nervous; I don't like exams."

Mari said to Asia, "Don't be nervous, you are even brighter than me."

Gideon said, "How is your dad? We are supposed to meet to discuss our next cricket match, but I've been quite busy at the building site. I might give him a call later."

Asia said, "Oh Mr LeBoun, my mum meant to ring you. Dad flew to India last night; Granddad is dying, so he had to travel in a hurry."

Gideon said, "Oh dear, I didn't know your granddad is ill?"

Asia replied, "Yes, he has cancer and went to the hospital for an operation four weeks ago; he's gotten weaker and weaker. He is sixty-five years old, so he might not survive."

Gideon said, "That's not old, sweetheart, your granddad is still very young. I hope when your dad gets there, your granddad will suddenly feel a lot better. Who knows seeing your dad might be just the tonic he needs."

They arrived at the school gate; Mari kissed her dad before she climbed down from the truck. Gideon leaned forward and waved good-bye; he shouted, "Good luck, girls; do you want a lift back, Mari?"

"No, Dad; Asia and I are going to the shops, and then I'm going back to her house; answered Mari."

Dad said, "Okay, let me know if you need a lift later; have a good day, and good luck girls!"

It was 8:45 when Mari and Asia entered the school yard; a few of her class mates were already waiting. Mari noticed Sonia was missing they walked straight over to Joan and Althea.

Mari said, "Hello, I hope Sonia isn't going to be late. If she is not on time, the exam supervisor won't let her take the exam."

Speak of the devil; they could see Sonia rushing down the street towards the school yard.

A few minutes later Sonia greeted the girls; "Hello all"

"You are just in time," replied Mari. "We were a bit worried you might miss out."

"Na; I hear it every day from Mammy and Daddy about the Christian High School being the best in St Vincent. So my parents made sure they woke me before they left this morning to go to open the shop."

Sonia's parents owned a grocery store at Abby Vale. They did a roaring trade, selling everything from provision yams and sweet potatoes to cornflakes and other imported food from America. They even sold mangoes when they were in season.

At 8:55, the exam supervisor, Mr Henry, came out into the school yard where the students had gathered. He stood on the doorstep and ushered the students to come in. Mari turned to her friends with her fingers crossed. "Good luck my friends I hope we are all successful," she said, clasping her hands and looking up to the sky. "Please God!"

The girls walked in and noticed the desks and chairs were not close together. Mr Henry asked the girls to be seated quietly and added, "No talking, please."

Mari and her clan sat in a row behind each other; Sonia sat first and the other four girls, Mari, Asia, Joan and Althea, in that order.

Mr Henry said, "Please note we do not allow anyone to use a calculator; if you are carrying one, raise your hand and I will keep it safe until the exam is over." Mr Henry muttered under his breath, "That's cheating as far as I'm concerned, and no way to pass an exam!

"Just one more thing; you are not allowed to leave the exam room except for medical reasons. So I hope you've visited the lavatory; if anyone needs to go, I can delay five minutes; anyone?"

He waited a minute none of girls took up his offer to use the lavatory. Mr Henry said to the class, "You have two hours; please make sure you take at least fifteen minutes to read through the pages; you are allowed to use the blank pages provided if you need to work out the arithmetic. Okay, you may begin."

At exactly eleven o'clock, Mr Henry said, "Your time is up; please stop writing and hand me your work on your way out."

First Island Cover Girl

After the exam ended Mari and her friends were all smiles; they were positive that they had done very well. The girls stood outside discussing some of the exam questions they were all excited that they had all of the answers from revision.

Mari promised her parents she would make her way home, but first she decided to stop by the café for something to eat. Sonia said; *oh what a brilliant idea*, the other girls decided to join them. They went to the café in Paul's Lott. Mari ordered ham sandwiches and a glass of mauby with ice and so did the other girls. An hour later, the girls left the café each licking choc ice lollies, except for Mari she'd bought her favourite, a sour sop lolly.

A few days before Mari's exam results were out Grandmother Dorothy noticed how anxious Mari looked. So, she reminded her granddaughter that the Melrose and LeBoun families were intelligent people. Mari told her grandma that the results would be posted on the notice board outside the school by the front gate.

"You have nothing to worry about," Grandma Dorothy said. "We are winners, you wait and see; on Thursday you will be over the moon."

On Thursday morning bright and early, Grandma Dorothy telephoned Annette; Mari answered the phone.

Grandma Dorothy said, "Hello sweetheart; how are you?"

Mari said, "I'm okay."

Grandma Dorothy said, "You don't sound okay. Is your mother taking you for your exam result?"

Mari said, "Yes, Mum is driving me."

Grandma Dorothy said, "Oh good. Ring me as soon as you get your good news, and stop worrying. Speak later . . . love you."

Mari said, "Love you too, Gran."

A few hours later, Mari rang her Grandma Dorothy. Her other Grandma was visiting; as soon as Mari's Grandma picked up the phone, she waved to her other Grandma Wilma to come and listen; she knew from Mari's happy voice that it was good news.

Mari said, "Guess what?"

"Grandma Wilma is here with me; answered Grandma Dorothy.

Mari said, "Hi Grans. I passed; I got 80 per cent!"

Grandma Dorothy said, "I told you that you had nothing to worry about."

"Wonderful! What about your friends?"

Mari said, "They all passed; all my friends are going to the Christian School for Girls. By the way, Gran, can you make our uniforms?"

"Yes, your Grandma Wilma and I will work through your summer holidays to get them ready."

♣♣♣♣♣

Just four weeks later, and on the last day of school before the holidays started. Mari and her friends were given a good send-off by Ms Cabral, their teacher. They would start at the new school after the summer holiday. The teacher baked a few cakes and brought several different kinds of juice. She also made lots of coconut cakes with pink colouring, Mari's favourite.

At two o'clock, everything stopped in Mari's class; some of her friends wanted to listen to music. But Ms Cabral would not have any of it, as some classes were still running. She did allow them to play a few games. They all complained that games were for kids.

Ms Cabral assured them that they would love the games she had in mind. One of the games they played was called charades.

The games they played were such a hit they didn't even notice the time passing; soon it was four o'clock, and the class couldn't remember ever having such fun. Mari and her friends walked out of the Paradise Primary School with goodwill messages written on their white blouses. Someone had written, "Miss you already," and many other good-bye signatures.

Chapter 11

Summer Holidays

On the first Monday of school summer holidays, Mari was more than happy to stay in bed until lunchtime. Her parents trusted her to look after her two younger brothers whilst they were out at work. Mari's parents were glad to put her in charge, as both sets of grandparents lived close by in the same village.

It was a lovely sunny morning, and her two brothers were playing netball in the front yard when Granddad Melrose drove up to the front yard in his Jeep.

"Hello children. Grandma is planning to go to the beach for a picnic today. Where is Mari?" Granddad Melrose realised it was a silly question. "She is still having her beauty sleep," he said, "but let me go check on her to see if she wants a day at the beach with us."

Granddad went upstairs to Mari's bedroom and knocked lightly on the door.

Mari shouted, "Go away!"

"Mari, it's me, your grandma sent me. She has planned a trip to the beach today with all the grandchildren."

Mari didn't hesitate; she shouted, "Oh, this is wicked!"

She rushed to the door to greet her granddad; she waved her arms, animated by the thought of a picnic on the beach. Mari was all excited; she said, "I love Grandma's picnics. Did she bake any cakes?"

"Yes, she has enough food to feed a big crowd."

Annice Browne

By that time Colin and Marvin came indoors; they were holding onto their granddad excitedly.

Colin asked, "Can we play volleyball too granddad?"

"Yes, your other grandparents are coming to the beach with us; we could play guys against the ladies." The boys would beat them any day; said Marvin.

Mari put on her bathing suit and covered it with a beach robe. She tied the polyester wrap material around her waist; it made a perfect skirt. Mari carried her transistor radio, and as far as she was concerned, she was ready for a day of fun.

Colin and Marvin got ready too; they were wearing sun hats and each carried a beach ball. They were very excited and couldn't wait to climb into granddad's jeep. Five minutes after they drove off, they stopped to pick up their cousins, Tony and Kia. They arrived at Grandma's house, and the children all got out and ran to the front door. Grandma Dorothy was excited too; she had packed the food into containers and was ready to load the jeep and go.

She had packed a selection of fruit juices, two large bags of ice cubes, and plenty of homemade snacks. Granddad made sure he packed a few beers, and they were ready to head to Sandy Beach. They arrived at noon; Josh, Wilma and grandson Danny had arrived and were already sitting on the beach, waiting for the Melrose family. With so many hungry children to feed, the grandparents decided to eat lunch before the fun on the beach began.

Granddad fetched the folding table, and the two Grandmothers laid out the feast of goodies. Mari and Kia spread the beach mats for everyone to sit and enjoy the delicious picnic feast that both Grandmas had prepared. Mari had turned her radio to full blast while they ate; they listened to music in the background. They all sat and admired the beautiful scenery; Granddads Josh and Malc pointed out the other Grenadine Islands outstretching on the far horizon. They also played games with the grandchildren to name the isles they saw in the distance.

After lunch, the granddads were stretched out on some beach mats and fell asleep and the two Grandmothers couldn't resist the warm turquoise sea water they went for a soak while the boys played volleyball. After thirty minutes, and their granddads woke up they organised a volleyball match, dividing into two teams, boys versus girls. Grandma Dorothy, Grandma Wilma, Mari, and Kai formed the girls' team, and

Malc, Colin, Marvin, Danny, and Tony were the boys' team; Josh was referee and told each team to position themselves, the shorter players in front and taller players at the back.

When they were all in position, he blew the whistle to begin play. The ladies were first to score, but after fifteen minutes of play, the two grandmothers became exhausted. Grandma Wilma told the teams she was too tired, and granddad Josh blew the whistle for a halftime break. "The hot sun has sapped all my energy," remarked Grandma Wilma as she lay out on the beach mat. See my children old age means that I need time out to rest and Grandma Dorothy agreed, she said; I am knackered too. They went off for a rest and they were replaced for the second half of the game. Malc refereed the game and Josh played with the girls' team. The match ended with—the boys' team scoring twenty goals to the girls' ten. When the match finished, Mari and Kia jumped into the turquoise sea for a long soak. They swam until Grandma Wilma said it was time to go home. But Mari and Kia were having too much fun; they shouted, "Oh no, we are not ready to go yet!"

The girls knew when they were beaten, and Grandma Wilma promised them they'd come again soon. Mari and Kia rode back in Grandparents LeBoun car, and the boys went with Grandparents Melrose. When they arrived home, Mari's mum was in the kitchen, preparing supper.

She invited her parents to stay for supper. Malc said he needed a quick shower. After supper, the family settled down to watch the James Bond film, *Goldfinger*.

The following week, Mari and her brothers travelled to Dorchester Village for a two-week visit at their great-grandparents Jack and Wendy LeBoun's home. They loved to spend time there, as their great-grandparents had a big shop and a big garden with lots of little fruit trees. There was also a tree house in the back garden; it was big enough for Mari to still climb into.

She often went there to get away from her noisy brothers or when the sun was too hot for her to bear. She would often sit high up in the tree house and write poems. She loved to write poems, and her aim was to have her poems published in a book. She often sat in the tree house thinking, *One day I will hold my own book . . . poems written by Mari LeBoun.*

Mari enjoyed the bountiful fruits in season during summer holidays from school. She ate various fruits, all from her great-grandparents'

LeBoun's garden. Mari also loved to accompany her great-granddad when he went to his farmland to harvest yams, dasheens, and sweet potatoes. She often asked him how he knew when it was time to dig up the vegetables. He told her that he never knew for sure if any of the vegetables were ready. But he usually had a slight idea from the time he planted them to how long it took to be fully grown; sometimes, the leaves would start to turn brown.

Mari's great-granddad told her that some vegetables took six months before they were fully grown. Sometimes the yam plant leaves turned very dry, and that was an indication that the yams were ripe underground. At night time, her great-grandparents used to sit outside the veranda and tell stories about the time when Britain was at war with Germany. Her great-granddad would say the public transportation wasn't working, so people had to walk to Kingstown. "Imagine walking now from Dorchester Village to Kingstown," Great-granddad LeBoun said, "about twelve miles away."

"We used to set out from home early morning at five thirty to go shopping in Kingstown. And we wore shoes made by a local shoemaker—it was tough leather, and on the journey to Kingstown we had to walk on a lot of gravel. By the time we reached Kingstown, my feet would be covered in blisters."

Mari was curious; she asked, "How did you walk back?"

Great-granddad said, "With great difficulty; sometimes the pain was so bad I had to walk barefoot; you children don't realise how lucky you are today!"

After the story telling, great-granddad started to sing; he always sang hymns, but soon he fell fast asleep in his rocking chair. It was almost as if he was singing himself to sleep.

The two weeks with Mari's great-grandparents passed quickly. Her mum and dad drove to the great-grandparents' house to fetch the children. It was amazing how agile they both were; they were in their eighties and still enjoyed the great-grandchildren visiting them on school holidays.

Mari was looking forward to going back home. She couldn't wait to see the uniform her grandmothers had made. The family arrived back home a bit late, so Mari rang Grandmother Dorothy first, and she told Mari that the uniforms were stitched and ready.

It was certainly a team effort; one grandmother made the blouses and the other made the skirts. The Christian School skirts were royal blue.

♣♣♣♣♣

Cousin Kia

Mari aunty Betsie lived next door with her husband Arnold, son Tony, and Kia. Mari often took turns to sleep over at her cousin's home at weekends. Mari always slept under a sheet, even though she lived in a tropical country. She said it was to protect her from mosquitoes; she'd cover her entire body from head to toe and just leave a spy-hole on her face to breathe.

Mari always insisted Saturday and Sunday mornings were for her extra lie-in; she told her family she needed her beauty sleep. She strongly believed it would repair skin cells and make her look more stunning if she slept well at the weekends. But her mum and her Grans would often say, "I don't know where this child gets her ideas about skin repairs. Does it work?"

♣♣♣♣♣

One day Annette was speaking with her niece Kia about the time when Mari was born.

Auntie Annette told her ten-year-old niece, "When Mari was born, Dr Malanki at the hospital said that she was a pretty baby. He said she would grow into a beautiful woman and one day she could be a film star. He went on to say he could imagine seeing her name in big letters just above the theatre entrance door: 'Starring Mari LeBoun!'"

Kia said, "Mari is light brown complexion, just like Uncle Gideon, and she has the same type of hair, which is soft and curly."

"Yes, but she's got her good looks from me: symmetric bone structure and two nice dimples to enhance her beauty; said Auntie Annette!"

Annette's older sister Betsie always fancied the best for her daughter Kia. She wanted her to be a paediatric doctor when she grew up. Betsie often said that St Vincent didn't have enough paediatric doctors. And not everyone could afford to travel all the way to Cuba when they fell ill.

Kia loved to read books; she was very bright in school, and Betsie imagined one day her daughter would make her very proud. She thought Kia would be ready to take the entrance exam next year at age eleven, when she could join her cousin Mia at the Christian Secondary School for Girls.

Chapter 12

Two Dwarves Down by the River

One day, Mari saw a dwarf woman washing her laundry down by the river; since then, she had hoped to catch another glimpse of her. So she often walked by the river near her home. She had never seen an adult that small before. She looked like a perfectly shaped woman with breasts, yet she was the height of a child.

The tiny woman Mari saw had green eyes and curly black hair. Whenever the woman saw Mari, she would race up the hill. Mari tried to follow her one day, but she could not keep up the pace, and the woman disappeared into the thick bushes.

Mari told Kia about the dwarf woman she met down by the river, but her cousin dismissed her account. She said, "Ah . . . you dreamt that!" So to solve the mystery, one day Mari invited Kia to accompany her down by the river after school.

One Friday evening, they both went to the river and sat on a big rock, patiently waiting for an hour, but they saw nothing.

After an hour had passed with no sighting, Kia continued to doubt Mari's story. She repeated to Mari, "You must have dreamt it," but Mari huffed at her cousin. She said, "It wasn't a dream!"

Kia answered, "We've been sitting here for an hour; do we need to sit here for a whole day? Do you know people often can have recurring dreams?"

Mari said, "It's not a dream, and I'm not mad either, the little dwarf is real. She is about three and a half feet tall with bow legs and breasts just like a woman—a little woman! She raced up that steep hill in a flash, and when I tried to follow her she disappeared; I think she hid away quietly in the bushes."

Kia said, "Do you believe in fairies?"

"No, and you shouldn't either," remarked Mari.

The girls decided to go home and planned to return the next day, on Saturday. The little lady might come to wash her laundry. Saturday morning, they hid behind a big rock stone, and after ten minutes, they could hear faint singing voices.

Kia said, "Did you hear that?"

Mari gently eased herself up from where she was stooping behind the big rock. She said, "Look, look, there is more than one woman!"

Mari and Kia waited until the little ladies were busy washing their clothes in the river. In the meantime, Kia apologised profusely to Mari for doubting her. She was in shock; she couldn't believe how tiny the women were. She had never seen any adults that small before.

Mari and Kia gave enough time for the ladies to settle down to wash their laundry before they introduced themselves. They stood up and slowly walked over to where the tiny ladies were busy washing their clothes. The lady that Mari had seen previously was about to run off. But the other woman stopped her and spoke to her in a language that neither of the girls had heard before.

Mari and Kia were walking on tiptoes so not to scare them away. Both girls were over five feet tall, and they towered over the two tiny ladies. The girls said, "Hello ladies . . ."

The older lady said to the younger lady, "*Dongo rungon, yungu stan-and dalagay* [Don't run, you stand here]!"

The younger lady hid behind the older lady. The older lady answered, "Mornin."

Mari asked, "What are your names?"

The older lady said, "*Mingee nay-aim-game* . . . Elsie [My name is Elsie]." Then she stepped aside to reveal the younger lady hiding behind her. She said, "*Dingis anga mengi sista . . . shegie . . . nay-m-game* Delcie. [This is my sister, her name is Delcie]."

Kia said, "Oh my God, they are speaking in their own language."

Elsie and Delcie could understand every English word Mari and Kia spoke. They spoke their own language because when the girls went to school all of the children treated them like freaks. When Elsie started school, the first week children followed her and taunted her. She became very unhappy and after a few years when Delcie started school the bullying got worse and both girls refused to go back to school. Their parents decided to protect Elsie and Delcie from such abusive behaviour, so they kept them at home.

The girls' parents were average height, both over five feet in height.

Mari and Kia were intrigued by what the ladies had to say so they wanted to know more about their little friends. They learned the ladies were twenty and eighteen years old and lived with their parents in a big pink house at the top of the hill. Mari and Kia knew this house well for its special design; it looked like something out of a story book. It had pink scallop designs around the roof, and the glass windows had rainbow floral designs.

Mari said, "I like your house, it is lovely to look at." Delcie said, "*Meigi daddy buildit* [My daddy built it]."

The ladies continued washing their clothes while Mari and Kia sat chatting with them. At ten o'clock Mari heard her mother calling her name; she stood up and told Kia she was supposed to go with her mum to the market. The girls waved good-bye and ran home.

Elsie and Delcie's parent had no time during the day to help them learn to read and write, as they were too busy working. So the girls formed their own vocabularies and invented their own dialect.

As soon as they turned teenagers, the two young ladies earned money making wicker baskets. Elsie and Delcie were gifted and blessed with a natural talent; they were able to create replicas of wicker baskets and table mats by just looking at them. They were very clever, as no one taught them the crafting skills they had learned.

Chapter 13

Cricket Match Tragedy

Malc and Josh were retired policemen, with time to do whatever they wished on a daily basis. "Tomorrow I am meeting the boys for a cricket match against the country boys; said Malc."

"Where are you playing the match?" asked Dorothy.

"The country boys' team are joining us at Dorchester Cricket Grounds. Do you want to come along?"

Dorothy knew straight away her husband would ask her to prepare food for the cricket match.

She thought at least if she prepared some food for him, he wouldn't expect her to go to his boring cricket match and sit all day, wondering what she could do better with her time.

So, Dorothy agreed to make a big sponge cake and other food that the team would enjoy. By the end of the day, Dorothy had baked enough food to feed an army. She loaded the food into plastic containers and piled them in the fridge to keep fresh and cool overnight.

Malc said, "Thank you, I know I can always rely on you to deliver. I'll get a few crates of beers on my way in the morning."

Dorothy said, "Can you win a cricket match if you are drunk?"

Malc replied, "A few beers won't make us drunk, it will make us play better."

On Wednesday morning, bright and early, Malc was up at eight o'clock. He showered before breakfast and then cooked himself the biggest breakfast. He made some peppermint tea freshly picked from his greenhouse.

Malc owned one of the best crops of herbs, and his greenhouse had a good supply for the whole family. He produced strawberries every year, and since the medical programme was broadcast over the radio, he has been known for topping the bill for producing good strawberries.

Malc told Dorothy, "Since that program you heard, everybody wants to taste strawberries." So, Malc was forced to build a high fence to stop thieves from entering his back garden at night. The thieves were in search of strawberries.

Early that morning Malc left in his jeep, laden with food, and his first stop was to load up the beers from Anu's shop, and then he collected Josh and Anu on his way to the cricket grounds. The morning was bright and sunny; Malc predicted hot weather; it is supposed to be at least 80° degrees by ten o'clock today.

Josh joked, "Well, I have my big hat to wear for shelter."

They all replied, "You look like a Mexican; that hat is far too big; how can you see the cricket ball coming towards you?"

Josh said, "What? The hat would be on my head, not covering my face!"

Malc said, "Professional cricketers wear helmets nowadays. It's a lucrative game so the players are more ferocious, they play to win and earn money."

The town team arrived at the cricket ground, and most of the country players were already there, with the exception of two players. At ten o'clock, when the match was supposed to begin, Malc turned his small transistor radio on to hear the news. The men were busy chatting away when the announcer said, "We have news coming in of a road accident . . .

"Two men on a motor bike collided with a truck carrying cement early this morning around nine o'clock at Goldimere Road. The two motor bike passengers died at the scene, and the truck driver sustained injuries that were not life threatening.

"The dead men's names have not been released, but the motor bike license number is . . . ; we believed they were travelling from Conari."

The men lamented, "Oh God, I think its Ivan and Dipa, but they were so young!" Dipa is Anu's brother . . . . and Anu went into a state of shock ... he almost fainted. Malc and Josh embraced Anu, to comfort him, while the other men sat with their heads bowed, and in total disbelief.

Malc said, "We have to abandon the match; God rest their souls." Then he walked to the cricket pavilion and telephone home to tell his wife the bad news. After he spoke to his wife he rang Anu's wife. Anu is Asia's dad, and she is Mari's school friend.

All the players fell silent; they looked overwhelmed by the sad news of their two team players.

Melvin, the country team captain, was first to speak; he said, "Let me ring Meena to see if she was listening to the radio news."

He dialled the number and Meena answered; she was distraught but managed to say the registration number was correct. "It's Ivan's motor bike; I can't believe Ivan and Dipa are garn!"

Ivan and Dipa had left in such high spirits; they were positive they would beat the town team today, but instead they have gone to heaven.

"How am I going to manage with two kids?" cried Meena. "Oh God ..." and the phone went quiet.

Melvin re-dialled the number; most of all he wanted to check that she was okay. This time his wife Shirley answered; she was actually with Meena when he rang. She reassured her husband that Meena was okay.

One of the country team players said, "You know, *it was only yesterday I said to them to ride with us, and Ivan said to me he was taking his motor bike. Dipa said, 'I will travel with you, Ivan!'*"

Melvin said, "That was their destiny; it is so sad. The two of them have young children; what an awful day. Life is so unfair!"

The men sat and chatted for more than an hour, but it wasn't lively conversation, mostly gloom and doom about freak accidents that had happened. When Malc checked his watch, it was 12:15. He said, "We might as well eat the food we have."

He fetched the ice bag with the mix of sandwiches, and salad. When he brought out a fold-up table, Josh said, "Dorothy thinks of everything, eh?"

He opened the table and spread out everything, together with paper plates. They didn't feel hungry, but they knew the extra energy would help.

Two hours later, instead of going home, they all decided to visit Ivan and Dipa's wives the two bereaved families. On the journey they decided to organise a dance and another cricket match to raise money for the families.

Firstly, they drove to Meena's home in Conari; Ivan's wife Maureen was also there, together with the entire village of neighbours. It was a terrible and morbid scene; two ministers were trying to comfort the families. Meena and Maureen looked drained and overcome with grief. The two team captains, Melvin and Josh, spoke with the wives and ministers present; they told them what they were planning to do. The ministers thought it was a brilliant idea and offered to help.

The town team left and drove back in total silence; no one spoke until they passed one of the lovely houses.

Josh said, "StVincent is a green place with some architectural splendour; look at that house. Man—that must cost a million dollars . . ."

Malc said, "Herbie Simmons lives there, alone with his wife. I used to go to grammar school with that guy. His children are in America but the grandchildren come on vocation every summer."

Josh broke the silence about the tragedy; he said, "We must order two wreaths shaped like cricket bats."

They all agreed; Josh said he could contact the florist to find out how much two wreaths would cost.

When Malc arrived home, Dorothy was waiting by the front step; she had heard the news on the radio as well. She opened her arms and hugged her husband.

She said, "I'm so sorry for those two families; how awful and Anu must be absolutely distraught his brother was so young. Mari went over to see Asia, and she can't stop crying. Come in, you looked drained."

Malc said, "I'll take a shower; I don't even feel hungry."

Dorothy replied, "I made some spicy soup with plenty of hot pepper."

"That will help me to relax," said Malc.

Next day Josh rang the florist to find out the cost of the two cricket bat wreaths. It was going to cost $150 in total. "So that's one hundred and fifty divided by twelve, so $12.50 each would cover the cost," he said. "The funeral is on Saturday; I was thinking we should wear our cricket uniforms."

Saturday morning at eight o'clock, it rained a bit but by ten o'clock the rain had stopped. The funeral was at two o'clock, so Malc told

Dorothy they would be setting out at twelve-thirty, travelling in Josh's mini bus.

When Josh's mini bus arrived at Conari, they all sat in the van outside the church for a little snack. People were already gathering, and they noticed everyone had the same idea about cricket uniforms, as mourners were all dressed in white.

The funeral cars arrived at the church. The families did their best to make the funeral service a celebration of Dipa and Ivan's short lives. But it was obvious to see they were absolutely grief stricken by the sudden loss. It was a sad, morbid day, and the entire island was plunged into grief. The cricket teams and close friends sang the hymn, "Abide with Me"; it was an emotional moment, and many mourners were in tears.

The following day, Malc felt very depressed; he hardly spoke a word, but Dorothy understood why. After lunch, he went to the cricket hall to meet team members for a few beers, and Dorothy thought it might help to numb the pain. When Malc left, he decided to walk to Josh's house. He normally drove, even though Josh's house was only a five-minute walk from his house. Dorothy always reminded him that he needed a bit of exercise.

They had organised two charity events: a dance and a televised cricket match; both tickets sold for $20. They had set a date for the following month to hold the cricket match, and the dance would be held in a fortnight's time. A publishing company kindly offered to print tickets and flyers for the two events. The families were very surprised at the amount of support they were given by everyone.

The night of the big charity dance came; it was held at Conari Methodist Church Hall. Raffle tickets were also sold; first prize was a bottle of champagne. It was a resounding success, as they sold $20,000 worth of tickets.

Several caterers volunteered their services to prepare food for sale. Dorothy and Wilma were responsible for baking cakes. They sold various cakes from small cupcakes to larger size family cakes. There were other items on sale and a mix of barbecue meals including roasted corns.

The charity cricket match was held at Abbey Vale Cricket Grounds. The match kicked off at ten o'clock and those who couldn't manage to attend tuned in on TV and radio. It was a picture perfect morning with blue sky; birds were flying, and a lively steel band entertained the crowd before the opening match began.

First Island Cover Girl

The players were obviously very nervous, as they have never played in a televised cricket match before.

Certainly, the cricket players were not accustomed to such a wide audience in front of spectators, TV cameras, and radio listeners. The event had turned into an island jamboree; both TV and radio announcers encouraged listeners to donate to the cause and give generously.

Meena and Maureen were amazed at the support they received from fellow Vincentians. They were inundated by the volume of well wishers and total strangers who generously offered their financial help.

It was a lively carnival atmosphere at Abbey Vale Cricket Ground: music, people dancing, and other spectators making loud noises and blowing vuvuzelas. Vendors sold every Caribbean food you can imagine.

The teams walked out on the playing field and were welcomed by a rapturous crowd. When the game ended, the country team won by twenty runs; it was a satisfying close to a very worthy cause. The following day, the donations were calculated and proceeds to the fund totalled $100,000. Later that day, the minister of sports Alvin Dingo went on TV and broadcasted a thank you message to the general public.

Here is the minister of sports' speech:

> *Good morning, fellow Vincentians. I am here to thank all citizens who gave their time and generosity to a worthy cause, and to inform you. I felt extremely proud of the way we united and managed to raise $100,000 for two young wives with four children to bring up singlehandedly. I urge everyone to continue to support them—this donation is our way of saying we felt their loss.*
>
> *Thank you once again.*

Later that day, the Alvin Dingo presented cheques of $50,000 each to Meena and Maureen at an informal gathering at the Conari Church Hall.

Chapter 14

Dorothy Melrose

Dorothy called at her daughter Annette's home one morning; the kitchen door was opened, so she walked in and shouted, "Annette?"

"Yes Mum, out here hanging up some clothes!"

"My dear, good morning, it looks like we are going to have another lovely sunny day. Annette, my God, do you wash clothes every day?"

"Mum, don't forget my husband is a builder; all of his jeans have paint stains. Gideon he hates dried-on paint stains, plus the kids need lots of clothes washed."

"Are you still coming with me to my appointment with Dr Dude?"

"Yes of course, what time is your appointment again?"

"We still have plenty of time more than an hour as my appointment is at ten-thirty."

"Okay, we'll take my car because I want to get some groceries in town."

Kingstown was only a twenty-minute drive away, and Dorothy often talked about the days when they used to walk to town on market day, carrying heavy load of vegetables on their head.

"What? With all those litres of drinks to buy, I won't be carrying those on my head."

"We used to carry provisions in big crocus bags; and after we sold the provisions, we used to buy groceries. So we walked into town with a load and returned with a load; hard work never killed anyone."

"That's what you think, Mother dear; people often drop dead—but I believe its hard work and hot sun; in some instances, it stops the heart, resulting in sudden death."

Around ten o'clock, Annette and her mum set off to the doctor's clinic; they arrived a few minutes earlier than planned because there was hardly any traffic. Dorothy walked into the surgery and announced her arrival to the receptionist.

"Good morning, Mrs Melrose to see Dr Dude."

The receptionist said, "Please take a seat, Mrs Melrose."

Annette and her mother sat right by Dr Dude's surgery door. Annette unzipped her bag and searched through her bag, and then she placed her left hand to her lips in wonderment.

"What's the matter, dear?"

Annette said; "I could have sworn I'd packed my book."

"What book is that?"

"The book title is *Memoirs of My Childhood*, by Annice Browne. It's an autobiography of her childhood growing up in the sixties in a village in the country."

"I can remember the sixties like it were yesterday; all that time some good ole days."

Annette said; "And Mum, I know you would find the book a nostalgic trip down memory lane."

"Oh that's good; it sounds right up my street."

"I could buy you a copy for your birthday; it's coming up soon."

Dorothy noticed a few copies of the Vincentian newspapers on a table in front of them. She picked up two copies and handed one to Annette. She remarked, "These are a few months old." The front-page story was "Man Killed Young Love."

"Oh, this is the sad case of that beautiful young lady hacked to death by a lunatic," Dorothy said. "Life is so unpredictable and fragile. I dread to think what her poor family must be still going through. This could happen to anyone; that's why I pray hard every day for my children to be safe."

"Mum, this is too painful to drudge up," remarked Annette. "God rest her soul!"

Dr Dude's surgery door opened and someone walked out, followed by the doctor. He called out the next patient's name: "Mr Pejo Walker?"

Dorothy said to Annette, "I thought it was my turn; I wonder how many more people is ahead of me? It's nearly eleven-twenty; the doctor must be running late, but no one ever tells us anything."

"Mum, at least we don't have anything pressing to do, we have an easy day today, and the grocery stores will still be opened when we finish here."

"Yes, that's true enough, but I just hate sitting in here. You don't know what virus is airborne in here."

"Oh Mum, you always have to think negative."

Mr Walker took only fifteen minutes with the doctor, and when he walked out of the surgery, the doctor called Dorothy's name. She jumped to her feet and entered Dr Dude's surgery quickly.

"Hello Mrs Melrose, how are you today? Keeping well?"

"Doctor, I get this dull pain from my hip on the right side right down to my foot; sometimes when I try to get up it is very painful. The other day I was standing in the post office queue (I don't know why they don't put benches for ole people to sit and wait), and my leg was extremely painful. My daughter Annette keeps telling me that I should use a walking stick, but people would be whispering all sorts about me if they saw me with a walking stick."

Dr Dude said; "Do you sit for long periods?"

"Yes, in the evening when I'm watching TV. I could sit down for at least five hours because I don't go to bed early; I'm retired. I've worked hard during my younger days. So now I can rest; and enjoy my own time."

Dr Dude said, "Mrs Melrose, there is nothing wrong with quality time, but you need to understand how the body works, and you are not getting any younger, so old pains could seize you up! What you need to do, especially in the evenings when you are relaxing, is after an hour sitting down, you must get up and walk around for at least ten minutes. You see, that would help the circulation too, because if you sit for a long period of time, then the old joints would seize up, and that is why you feel dull pain in your hip and leg.

"Let's check your blood pressure; which arm do you prefer?"

Dorothy stretched out her right arm and the doctor fitted the blood pressure band above her elbow."

"Lord Jesus, this is too tight!"

Dr Dude said, "I know, but it has to be tight to give a better reading. I'm sorry."

Dorothy kept still for the time. Then Dr Dude looked at the blood pressure monitor reading; he said, "Your blood pressure is a bit high, 157/90. Are you taking your tablets regularly?"

"Yes, Doctor," replied Dorothy.

"I think I would try another tablet, and then after two weeks I would like you to have a blood test. Please book an appointment with Nurse Megerson. She will take your blood and send it to the hospital lab. Give it another week and book an appointment to see me for the results of your blood test. Do you have any more questions, Mrs Melrose?"

"No, Doctor," replied Dorothy.

The doctor handed the prescription to Dorothy and bid her a good day.

As soon as Annette saw her mum, she stood up and asked her if everything was okay.

Dorothy replied, "The doctor has changed my blood pressure tablets, and he said I shouldn't sit for more than an hour without getting up and moving about to help blood circulation. After an hour, I should get up and walk around for at least ten minutes." You should take heed mum; replied Annette.

Annette and her mum left the clinic and walked to where the car was parked, and they noticed how hot the sunshine was from the time when they arrived just before ten-thirty.

As they entered the car, it was baking hot. Annette turned the engine on and turned the air conditioner to full blast then she drove off towards Kingstown. It was lunchtime, so they stopped off at the Sunrise Café for a bite to eat.

The café was full, not an empty seat in sight. Annette told her mother to keep a look-out for an empty table or they would have to eat lunch sitting in the stuffy car. After ten minutes standing in the long queue, Dorothy spotted a family leaving a table of four empty seats; she quickly walked over to the vacant table.

A woman with four children behind her approached Dorothy. She had long false fingernails and false eyelashes that made her resemble a cow. The woman was wearing a short mini skirt, revealing a pair of legs as big as tree trunks. The woman's head swayed aggressively, and she raised her hand and said, "Missus, I've been waiting thirty minutes for a table, so move right out of my face!"

Dorothy knew better not to argue with a woman like that, so she walked right back to where Annette was waiting in the queue. Annette said, "This world is full of ignoramuses. I'm glad you had the sense to walk away. I know how quickly things can get out of hand, but anyway it's her turn to be seated with her children."

Mum said, "Let's hope her children belong to the same dad. Women nowadays make babies like they are free, and I don't know how some of them manage to keep them, let alone educate them. Look at Ruby next door; she's got six, and lucky thing all of them are boys so they don't need much clothes; they only wear short trousers at home.

"As to the father, that Cliff Matthews is in and out of jail; he's quite a criminal. If it wasn't for the granddads, I don't know if Ruby could have managed to raise her boys, but somehow she manages to send them all to school. Come Monday morning, you would not recognise them; their shoes are as shiny as a mirror and smartly dressed in uniform.

"The oldest is only thirteen; there is Desmond, Leroy, Kenrick, Godwin, Aaron, and Cedric, and their mother is only twenty-nine. She started making babies at the age of sixteen; she was such a quiet teenager, it was a shock to her parents when she fell pregnant. She used to go to Immaculate School in town and then fell in love with that waster.

"Ruby and Cliff Matthews got married at the courthouse in Kingstown recently. She is now Mrs Ruby Matthews. It wasn't anything big, just the children and a few family members. But recently, Ruby's husband has turned his life around; he hasn't been to jail for two years now. He is a reformed Christian at the Streams of Power Church."

Chapter 15

Mari Secondary School

The school holidays were over and Mari was ready for secondary school. Monday morning bright and early, Mari's dad was sitting outside in the truck, waiting to give her a ride to school. School started at nine o'clock, and Mari was a little nervous; she always felt nervous when she was doing something new.

As soon as Mari arrived at the school gate, she saw Sonia, her friend, who had just arrived too. She kissed her dad, who waved good-bye and said, "Have a nice day, sweetheart."

But Mari was too excited to answer her dad; she ran straight to Sonia. The first hour of her new school began with a morning service in the school hall.

The principal introduced all the head of class teachers; Mari's teacher was Mrs Grabrel, a white lady from England. After morning service finished, the new students followed Mrs Grabrel. There were forty students in the class. Mari made sure she was sitting close to her friends Sonia, Asia, Joan, Althea and Rosemary DeFratus is Mari's new friend; they all sat in the third row. Mrs Grabrel introduced herself and said that she had lived in St Vincent for ten years with her husband and three boys. Her sons were twelve, fourteen, and sixteen, and her youngest son had just started at St Jacob's School.

She went on to say she knew how the new girls felt today. She assured the class that she would make every effort to help them to enjoy their time in her class. Mrs Grabrel asked the class to introduce themselves by telling their name and where they lived.

When it was Mari's turn to speak, she said, "Hello, my name is Mari LeBoun and I'm twelve and a half years old. I have two younger brothers, Colin and Marvin. I live at Paradise Village."

After everyone had introduced themselves, Mrs Grabrel said, "Well, you all have beautiful names; please bear with me, as it may take a few weeks to register all the faces with the names. I will be teaching you English; here is a list of your other teachers."

She handed out a sheet with the names of the other teachers.

"I am taking your class all day today," she continued, "as we have a lot to go through. For your first task, I would like you all to write me a short account of your summer holidays."

Mari thought *oh this is great; I am happy to write about my summer in the country with great-grandparents LeBoun*. She wrote:

> My brothers and I spent two weeks of our school summer holidays at Dorchester Village with our great-grandparents. They have run the LeBoun Grocery Store in the village for over forty years.
>
> Our great-grandparents are Jack and Wendy LeBoun in their late eighties and still very strong and agile. They've employed two shop assistants to help serve customers, and I love to spend time at the shop. Grandma has showed me how to use the till, and I have served a few customers. Gran said it is a good experience for me to learn how to calculate money. I loved every minute of it, especially greeting and serving customers.
>
> My great-grandparents have a little pig farm; they raise pigs and sell the pork meat to customers. I like the little piglets. But the more mature ones eat all day long and use their mouths to plough mud. Also, there is a tree house in the garden . . . I call it my hideaway. I normally climb into the tree house and sit quietly and write poems. One day I would love to publish a book of poems. Summer is fun; we go to the beach for picnics with our family.

Chapter 16

Friends Reunited

Mari was enjoying her new life in secondary school. However, she didn't appreciate the fact that her parents drove her to and from school every day. She was quite envious of her friends, who rode the school bus. So one day her dad drove her home from school, she told him that she would prefer to catch the school bus with her friends, because she felt that she was missing out on the social aspects.

Mari's dad said, "What? Why would I pay a school bus to transport you to and from school when I could do it for free? And if I can't fetch you from school, your mother or grandparents would. Darling, you don't know how privileged you are; some of your friends' parents would swap with you any day, in order to save money."

Mari was not surprised that her father had said this, and she felt guilty for even suggesting it to him. Then she realised there are many students who travelled more than twelve miles each day, which was quite an expenditure plus school fees and lunch money on a daily basis. So Mari realised she was privileged and promised her dad never ever to complain again!

Mari sat in silence as she drove home in her dad's truck; she felt so guilty when she realised that one of her best friends lived so far from the school. Rosemary DeFratus travelled from Georgetown, about eighteen miles, every day to attend Christian Secondary School. Mari turned to her dad and said, "Maybe I could help Rosemary. Can she stay at our home during the school term?"

Mari's dad told her it was a good idea but she would need to speak to her mum. After that they would have to meet with Rosemary's parents to discuss accommodation plans.

Later that evening, Mari explained her bright ideas to her mother. Mari told her that she didn't realise how lucky she was to live only twenty minutes away from school.

Mari said, "Could Rosemary lodge with us during school term?"

Mari's mum said she would be happy for Rosemary to stay Monday through Thursday, and she could travel home on Friday evenings.

The next day at school, Mari told Rosemary about her plan. Rosemary could not believe her luck, as her parents were wondering the same thing just a few days ago. Rosemary told Mari her parents would be extremely grateful if she didn't have to travel daily from Georgetown to school.

It was Thursday evening, and as soon as Rosemary arrived home, she rushed to her mother and told her that Mari had offered to put her up Monday through Thursday each week during the school term, and then she would travel home on Friday. Rosemary added, "Mari's parents would like to meet Dad and you to discuss the arrangements." Later that evening, Vinola, Rosemary's mother, telephoned Mari's mum Annette.

Mari answered the phone when it rang, and the lady at the other end asked, "Is that you, Mari?"

"Yes, this is Mari . . ."

"It's Rosemary's mum, Vinola."

Mari said, "Oh hello Mrs DeFratus. I'll get my mum for you."

Mari passed the phone to her mum and told her who it was.

"Hello Vinola, my name is Annette . . ."

"Wait a minute", Vinola said; "is that you, Annette Melrose?"

Annette said, "My goodness; I recognise this voice . . . are you Vinola Jackson? You went to Girls High School, right? But we were in a different class?"

"Yes, you were a year ahead of me."

"Well, I'll be damned, what a small world . . ."

"No, you mean what a small island!"

They both laughed.

"So who are you married to?" Annette asked.

"I married Lennox DeFratus, my childhood sweetheart."

Annette said, "Who is Lennox DeFratus again? The name rings a bell."

"Do you remember Laverne DeFratus, who went to Girls High School? She was a few years older than us."

Annette said, "Yes, red hair and freckles; she was Deloris Hairwood's best friend."

"That's right; and Laverne is Lennox's big sister."

Annette said, "Yes, I remember all of them; so he got you in the end. I remember how you gave him a hard time. I'm married to Gideon LeBoun . . . oh yes, the LeBoun from Paradise Village."

"Well, I can't believe this." After chatting awhile, she arranged to come on Sunday evening to discuss Rosemary boarding at Mari's home.

Annette said, "Of course, and Rosemary could bring her things and stay overnight for school next day."

"Oh wonderful; I'll see you soon then . . . bye bye!"

When Annette hung up the phone, she said to Gideon, "You won't believe this, Rosemary's parents are Vinola Jackson and Lennox DeFratus."

Gideon said, "Really? I went to St Jacob's School with Lennox DeFratus; well, well, it will be nice to see them again!"

Friday morning in school, Mari and Rosemary's topic of conversation was about their parents, who were old school friends—reunited.

Rosemary said, "This makes it even better for me to stay at your home; at least your parents are not strangers to my parents."

♣♣♣♣♣

On Sunday evening at four o'clock, Rosemary and her parents pulled up in their car outside Mari's front yard. Gideon and Annette were standing by the front door to greet their long-lost friends. They were so pleased to see each other and had so much catching up to do. By the time Vinola and Lennox left, Mari and Rosemary were fast asleep in their beds.

Rosemary was given the small spare bedroom, and she had her own en-suite bathroom. She thought this was an absolute luxury. Vinola warned her daughter to keep the room tidy and behave herself in the LeBouns' household.

Both parents agreed that Rosemary could stay at the LeBouns' home from Monday through Thursday and return home on Friday evening. Rosemary's dad promised to collect her every Friday and bring her back either Sunday evening or Monday morning. Rosemary became Mari's twin sister; they were inseparable. It worked very well too with her parents, because Gideon and Annette resumed their close friendship with Vinola and Lennox. They took turns organising parties and barbecues, alternating homes. Vinola was a nurse at Georgetown Hospital, and Lennox was a telecommunications engineer.

Lennox spoke at lengths with Gideon about telecommunications being the new way forward; he mentioned that many people were getting their own telephones in homes. He wondered how society could manage without home telephones. He said the next big media connection would be a television in every home.

Gideon said, "Only the rich and middle class people can afford a TV."

Lennox said, "You haven't got that problem."

Gideon laughed and said, "Neither have you!"

Lennox continued the conversation; he said, "Computers are getting smaller too. The ones they use at the airport and the electrical power stations are much smaller than those mainframes they used before. The old mainframes were like a huge cabinet.

"I might learn about computer technology; it seems to be the new way forward in telecommunications. My job is similar but it's just not as big as computer programming."

In the meantime, Annette and Vinola were chatting about their school days. They were going through a roll call of names from classes at their old school. Quite a few of Annette and Vinola's school friends were now living in Canada or America. They both kept in touch with different friends, so it was good to exchange information about people they both knew from school. By the time Lennox and Vinola left, it was very late, but they all agreed it was a wonderful reunion.

Annette told Rosemary right from day one that she would expect her to do the same chores as Mari. But Rosemary was more than happy with her new arrangements; she didn't expect any less, as she wanted to be a part of the family. She even ironed her own school uniform.

Each day the two girls took turns to wash dishes, sweep the yard, folded the laundry, and clean their bedrooms. Mari and Rosemary often sat at the dining table to finish their homework. It was mostly writing essays and memorising poems; when they needed to read an English literature book, the girls would sit alone in their bedrooms for quietness.

After homework, Mari, Rosemary, and Kia played hopscotch in the yard. Gideon had painted a permanent hopscotch table in the yard, and Mari's brothers also had their own netball game with the basket hanging on the wall in the other corner of the yard.

Rosemary felt like one of the family; she even called Mari's parent "auntie" and "uncle." Mari and Rosemary were inseparable; she was the sister Mari never had, and Rosemary, who had two younger sisters, was very happy to oblige. Rosemary felt very privileged to stay with the LeBoun family during the school term.

Lodging with the LeBoun family during school terms certainly helped her parents financially, so they were forever grateful to Mari's parents.

Mari knew how privileged she was to have a best friend, a playmate the same age who attended school with her. They shared the same friends in school, and they could talk about boys too. The St Jacob's School for Boys was adjacent to the Christian Secondary School for Girls. Mari and Rosemary often talked about the boys they admired.

♣♣♣♣♣

At the age of fifteen, Rosemary and Mari's relationship turned sour briefly when they both fancied the same boy. The boy's name was Deshaun, and Mari told Rosemary he had winked at her. But Rosemary was convinced he had winked at her first. The following day at lunchtime, the girls were walking back to school when they saw Deshaun with two other friends. Rosemary challenged Mari to say hi to Deshaun, so she willingly agreed.

As they approached Deshaun and his friends, Mari walked up to him and said, "Hi Deshaun."

Deshaun said, "Hi Mari," and then he waved at Rosemary, who was standing alongside Mari, but the girls noticed he had winked several times as he stood there talking to them.

Mari couldn't stop laughing, as she realised Deshaun's wink was an unusual habit; as he did it unintentionally.

Mari and Rosemary agreed that they felt no chemistry for Deshaun, so they made up and gave high fives. Friends . . . . you bet!

Chapter 17

Annette's New Career

Annette looked through the local newspaper and found a job advert for a teacher's post. She read the job description and remembered the conversation she had a few months with Mari, and she had encouraged her mum to enrol at the Teachers' Training College.

So later that day, Annette mentioned her plans to her husband; she told him she was thinking of changing jobs.

Gideon said, "Oh, what would you like to do instead?"

"I always wanted to be a teacher, but I would need to attend college."

"How long do you need to attend college?"

Annette said, "I am not certain, but I could find out."

"Go for it, sweetheart; the business is doing okay, so finance wouldn't be a problem."

The next day Annette rang the Education Department in Kingstown. The lady on the telephone told her to pick up a prospectus at the Kingstown Library. The lady told her that she would need to hurry if she wanted to begin the new term, which started in September.

Annette went to the college to register for the two-year teachers' course. She knew right from the start that it wasn't going to be an easy task. But she knew with three students (four, counting Rosemary) at home, they could all work together and share knowledge. So every evening when the children sat down to finish their homework, she would do the same.

By December, Annette was well into her first term at college. She couldn't believe how much she was enjoying her studies; she even joined the tennis club and played tennis once a week.

One of her workshop exercises included anger management, school bullying, and first aid. It was an eye opener for Annette, and she realised it was beneficial to her as a parent to know the ins and outs of dealing with unruly children.

Annette soon had only one term left before graduation. It was an intense period; she was busy revising all day for her exams and through the early hours of the next morning. She had just one more paper to complete, and while she was busy studying, her mother rang. There was bad news in the family. Malc's ninety year-old father Claudius Melrose, Annette's grandfather, died suddenly from a heart attack.

Annette was absolutely devastated at the loss of her loving granddad. The next morning, she went with a grieving mind to college and sat for her final exam. Even though she was sad, she couldn't help but notice how calm and relaxed she felt as she sat in the exam hall. She felt her granddad was looking over her, supporting her dreams.

Annette waited six long weeks for her exam results. Gideon was right by her side when she collected her results at the college. They stood outside the exam hall; she held the sealed brown envelope nervously as her husband looked on, but she was so nervous her hands were shaking. Gideon reached out and pulled Annette close to her.

He said, "Hon, whatever the results, it won't be from lack of hard work. I am right behind you. Anyway, you've worked really hard and I'm sure it's good news; go on, open it."

Annette slipped one finger under the sealed envelope; she said, "Well, here we go!" She quickly scanned through the results list; she had passed all six papers. She was so happy she began to cry.

"Hon, this calls for a celebration tonight. I'm so proud of you! We should have a big barbecue with all the family. God knows we need this to uplift our spirits after Granddad passing and we need to cheer up Grandma Doreen."

A few weeks later, Annette applied for a primary school teacher's post at Paradise Village, the same school her eight-year-old son Marvin attends. When he realised his mother was going to teach at his school, he didn't welcome that idea one bit.

Marvin said, "Are you going to teach my class, Mammy?"

Annette said, "No sweetheart; I wouldn't be so cruel to you. Don't worry."

Marvin said, "It's not that I'm ashamed of you but I don't want you to teach me; my friends would tease me if you do."

Annette said, "I know, son, you have nothing to worry about; I will be teaching younger students. I love you very much and wouldn't want you to be unhappy."

Marvin said, "I'm proud of you, Teacher LeBoun!" Then Marvin hugged and kissed his mother and ran to the front yard, where his brother Colin was playing basketball with friends.

Chapter 18

Carnival Beauty Queen

Mari still had the ambition to be the world's first Caribbean supermodel. Mari often said she had big plans; and she wanted her accomplishments to spread worldwide, America and Europe. She commented that with a surname like LeBoun, she could take advantage of the family's French connections and theatrical surname.

Grandma Wilma replied, "Yes, as slaves, maybe your grandfather's ancestors were probably owned by the LeBouns. In those days slaves were given their masters' surnames."

Mari replied, I bet!

"My aim is to help all beautiful black women with the same ambition to pursue their fashion modelling dreams; I want to be a role model for Caribbean beauties."

Mari's grandma said, "There's nothing wrong with having dreams, but yours are over the top. Have you ever seen a Caribbean beauty on the world famous catwalk?"

Mari said and ignoring her grandma, "Oh, I would love to travel the world."

"Mari if you work hard in school; you could be anything, but modelling is just a dream, my child!"

At twelve years of age Mari was already five feet, eight inches tall, and both set of grandmothers often said, "Those full lips make you have too much to say! Go and pick up your book, reading books can broaden the mind and make you intelligent."

Grandma said, "There are so many things you could do if you pass your exams in school; you could be a nurse like your Aunty Betsie."

"Everybody loves Betsie; she is well respected all over the island, and people even recognise her when she travels to Bequia and Mustique; you can't want more than that for accomplishment in life."

Mari assured her grandmas, "I will be the first Caribbean supermodel; you wait and see!"

She was standing with her arms wide opened and glaring eyes.

Mari said, "My face will appear in all of the American magazines; I will travel to London, Paris, and Milan."

♣♣♣♣♣

Mari and Rosemary were about to turn seventeen; Mari's birthday was in June and Rosemary's was in July. The girls also were looking forward to graduation day at the end of secondary school.

The graduation gowns were royal blue and cost $20 to rent for the evening. The event kicked off at five o'clock in the school hall; there were over two hundred parents, grandparents, and siblings all seated in the audience.

The school principal, Mr Aiden Rooster, and Mrs Erica Blueberry, a member of the ministry of education, presented diplomas to the graduating students. When it was Mari's turn to collect her diploma, her mother whispered to her dad, "She looks like a catwalk model already. I didn't realise how tall and stunning our daughter has grown."

Mari's dad said, "We are both beautiful people, with beautiful children!"

Mari walked up to the principal, shook his hand, bowed, and took her diploma. Her entire family stood up to cheer her. Colin and Marvin made whistle sounds; all the family was so happy and proud.

Now that Mari had completed secondary school, she had to begin another chapter in her life: either further education or do something else.

Two months later, Mari enrolled at the local college for a three-month secretarial course.

Mari enjoyed her time at college and made new friends, but she still wanted to pursue a career as a model in the fashion world. She hated the idea of sitting in front of a keyboard typing all day, but she also knew that it would be good to learn to type.

Six months later, Mari was reading through the local newspaper and noticed an advert. It read, "Beauty queen for this year's carnival." Mari showed it to her mum and asked, "Mum, could I enter this beauty queen competition?"

"Yes, what do you need to do?"

Mari said, "It said contestants have to be between seventeen and twenty-one."

"Well, give it a go and see what happens!"

Mari said, "Mum, I would need to have some professional photos taken."

"We could get some done in town. Let's check with your father first to see if he approves of you taking part in the Carnival Queen competition."

Later that evening, Annette asked Gideon if he would mind if Mari entered the St Vincent and the Grenadines Carnival Queen competition. Gideon had no problems with that, he said, providing they also attend the events. He said, "I don't want unscrupulous people taking advantage of our daughter."

The next day, Annette accompanied her daughter to the photographic studio in Kingstown, and they were told that the photos would be ready next day. Mari couldn't wait to collect the photos the next day, and Rosemary went with her to the photo studio.

The man at the studio handed Mari a large brown envelope; she was so excited she opened it instantly. There were four A4 size photos of Mari. At the photo shoot, Mari wore a purple dress with six big silver buttons down the front and grey sandals to match.

Mari said, "Oh my God, are these really me?"

Rosemary put one arm over Mari's shoulder to admire the photos; she turned to Mari and said, "Wow, these are beautiful, but then you're very pretty."

Mari turned to Rosemary, smiled, and said; "you're pretty too!"

They were both right, in fact, they could pass for sisters; they looked so alike. Mari kept looking at the photos.

Half an hour later, they caught the mini bus home and stopped off at the Paradise Primary School, where Mari's mum worked. When they arrived in the classroom, Mari noticed her mother was busy. So they waited a few minutes until she was free. In the meantime, Mari could see the eagerness on her mum's face; she couldn't wait to look at the photos.

As soon as Annette took one of the photos out from the envelope, she remarked, "Wow, my beautiful young lady! I would love to frame that one . . . and this one . . . oh, they are all lovely. Just wait till your grandmothers see these!"

Later that day, Mari went to visit her grandparents LeBoun and she met her other grandparents who were visiting too. She showed the photos to them; the look on their faces they showed so much pride at Mari's stunning beauty and couldn't stop admiring the photos. "She is turning into a beautiful young lady," they all remarked.

Mari's grandfathers raised concerns about beautiful young women being exposed to men with bad intentions.

Grandma Wilma said, "We can't wrap her up in cotton wool, you know, and anyway, she's been raised with good morals, so we are not worried."

Grandma Dorothy added, "A lot of time young women behave naughty because of the way they were brought up. I have every trust in our granddaughter; we've given her good guidance, and we wouldn't expect anything less than for her to conduct herself with respect and dignity."

♣♣♣♣♣

Four weeks later, Mari received a call from the carnival organiser, Joyce Allstar. She invited Mari to attend an informal interview and asked that she bring along some snap shots of herself. Mrs Allstar told Mari that contestants would be expected to take part in a catwalk show wearing a bikini followed by an evening gown.

Mari's mum accompanied her to the interview. Mrs Allstar explained the procedures of the carnival queen competition, and Annette felt reassured, as it was a well-organised event.

The Carnival Queen competition was televised on Saturday evening, July 23rd 1988. Mari was a little nervous and a little negative prior to the event. All she could think about was that so many people would be watching her. Mari thought, *suppose I slip walking down the stairs; what if I don't know the right intelligent answers to give the interviewer?"* These thoughts went through Mari's mind, giving her nervous butterflies sensation in her stomach.

Rosemary knew Mari too well and told her to get rid of all negative thoughts in her head and go out there to win the competition.

She said, "Think of all the exposure you are going to get in just an hour of parading as a beauty pageant."

As the audience gathered at the theatre, it was certainly a busy evening; there were vendors selling snacks. A lady was even selling wicker baskets; Dorothy and Wilma noticed her as they walked into the theatre.

The vendor shouted, "Get your baskets, lovely baskets." She held one up as Dorothy and Wilma walked by; she said, "This one is nice to put your groceries in."

Dorothy said, "I'll buy one later, thank you!"

The theatre was packed to capacity; all of Mari's family and friends were gathered in the audience. Mari and eleven other contestants were backstage. First they would go on stage wearing bikinis. One by one the young beauties were introduced to the audience by the presenter.

Mari was number eight; she came on stage holding a microphone in her hand, looking a bit nervous but absolutely stunning.

"Hello," she said, "my name is Mari LeBoun from Paradise Village, and I'm seventeen years old."

Then she walked off, and all the family stood up to clap.

After the twelve contestants had finished parading in bikini outfits, there was a ten-minute interlude. During that time the king of calypso, the Mighty Sparrow, entertained the audience with two of his favourite songs.

Following the second segment of the show, the beauty queens came on stage wearing evening gowns. Mari walked on stage wearing a maxi dress her mum had bought from one of the boutique shops in town. The dress was pink with silver sequins and a big silver belt; she wore silver shoes to match. Her hair was brushed up with curls bunched together and a fringe; she looked like a beauty queen. After another interval, a live calypso band played to entertain the crowd. At the end of the interval, the music stopped and the presenter addressed the audience.

The presenter said, "This has been a fierce competition, and it was difficult to pick three winners. I believe they are all beautiful, intelligent young ladies. They were rated not just for their beauty but for personality and intelligence. We now have the results of the Vinci Carnival Beauty Queen competition; here are the third, second, and first place winners."

When Mari heard who won third, she thought, *I haven't got a chance*. Then the runner-up was announced, and Mari thought; *"I'm sure that girl looks prettier than me"*. And then the presenter said, "The winner of the 1988 Carnival Beauty Queen of St Vincent and the Grenadines is . . ." There was a pause as the ten remaining beauties held hands, standing in a circle nervously.

Then he announced her name: "Mari LeBoun!"

Everyone began cheering the winner. Mari put her hands to her mouth; shaking nervously, she kept saying, "Oh my God . . ." Then she was ushered to the stage. As she walked to the centre, cameras flashed; she glimpsed her family waving their arms joyfully.

Mari was ushered to a big chair on the stage; she thought it looked like the throne for the queen of England. Mari sat down and the prime minister's wife placed the crown carefully on her head, and everyone clapped; most of the audience were standing. By that time her proud parents were on stage with Mari.

Mari was immediately swamped by TV presenters wanting to interview her. The judges, from St Vincent, Barbados, and Trinidad, were interviewed next, and then it was her parents' turn to speak on television.

After they were interviewed, Mari's mum said to her dad, "I forgot to set the video to record the show."

"There is no need to worry mum set her video so we could get a copy done for us. We need to keep it for Mari to show her children—our grandchildren one day;" replied Annette.

Chapter 19

Supermodel—Mari LeBoun

Mari's career went from strength to strength after winning the carnival beauty queen competition. Her ambition to become a fashion model began to look more realistic. She was getting work from magazines and for TV advertising. When Mari was eighteen, she thought maybe there was more she could do to expand her career.

She decided to book her name at a modelling agency in New York. She mailed her portfolio and thought no more of it. Then a month later, she received a telephone call inviting her to an interview in New York. Her mum agreed to travel with her.

The interview went very well, and she was invited to take part in photo shoots; it was the custom for the modelling agency to circulate photos to boutique companies and fashion designers in America. Mari and her mum returned home after two weeks in New York.

Gideon was waiting when they arrived at the airport. He had some good news for his daughter. He said, "Nice to see you are both back safely, but this morning the modelling agency called, and they want you to travel right back to New York."

Mari asked when; her father replied in two days time. Then he handed her a piece of paper, which had the flight details, contact name, and a telephone number. She turned to her parents, and her dad said, "It's okay; you go and pursue your dreams! I know that it's far away, darling, but we are always at the other end of the telephone if you need us."

Mari flew back to New York and was met by the modelling agency rep at JFK Airport.

She was driven to a hotel in Manhattan, and there were four other girls staying there. The lady who collected Mari from the airport introduced her to the three friendly American girls; they were named Isabella, Kate, and Eloise.

Mari made sure she telephoned home, as she knew her family would worry. After reassuring her family that she was okay, it was down to business. They had to go straight to an induction meeting.

The meeting room was set up just like an office, with a big table and chairs. The girls were asked to introduce themselves in turn; when Mari introduced herself, they wanted to know more about St Vincent.

One of the mentors, Gertude, asked Mari if St Vincent had any good locations suitable for photo shoots. Mari recommended Bequia or Mustique for lovely, picturesque locations.

Soon Mari and her companions were flying back to Mustique; ten people took the flight: the three girls she met, two mentors, and four photographers. Mari's dad met them at the Airport and invited them to a barbecue. After the photo sessions, they all went to Mari's home.

Gideon and Annette's garden was very big, so the barbecue party went very well that evening with plenty of food, drinks, and music; they partied into early Sunday morning.

After the group left, Mari's parents felt at ease that they'd met the people who would be helping their daughter's career.

Annette said, "Gertude seems very grounded and mature."

"Let's hope your first impression is correct, but we've brought our daughter up well," replied Gideon.

Three months passed, and Mari's career was growing from strength to strength. She called her parents from New York and told them her exciting news: she would be on the cover of one of America's leading magazines. Mari promised to mail a few copies of the magazine to her family back home in St Vincent. This was truly her dream come true.

A few days later, Mari received the magazines; she was overjoyed and bursting with pride. The front-page headline read, "First top model and stunning beauty from the tiny island of St Vincent and the Grenadines: Mari LeBoun."

Mari kept admiring her photo on the cover of the magazine. In retrospect, she remembered how much her grandparents tried to dissuade her from pursuing that career. She realised instantly she was right to follow that dream.

Mari was earning $6,000 a month, a huge salary in her opinion. Even though her parents were well off, she was able to give financial support to her two brothers. Each month, she transferred half of her salary into an account in St Vincent to help fund her brothers' education.

After a few years, Mari was one of the top models; she was ranked the fifth model in the world. She had her own apartment in New York and attended college part-time, studying law, because she remembered her mum told her education was the key to success.

During her time at college, she met a handsome young man named Pier Dior. His parents were very rich; they owned a big shipping company exporting cars to South America from New York. Mari was head over heels in love with Pier.

He even accompanied Mari to some of her photo shoots. He couldn't bear to be apart from her; whenever she had to travel to different states in America, Pier would go with her.

Chapter 20

Mari's Engagement

Pier's parents were Brazilians, and after a year and a half of dating Mari, he travelled with Mari to meet his extended family in Brazil.

The day they took the flight, Mari was a bit nervous. When she arrived at the airport, she wondered if Pier's grandparents would understand English. She was too shy to ask Pier so she kept her fears a secret. Mari and Pier were picked up by a chauffeur-driven car and taken to Pier's grandparents' home.

The journey from the airport took an hour; when they arrived, Mari couldn't believe how big and beautiful the houses were on the street where Pier's grandparents lived. Pier's family lived in a massive house with a big electric iron front gate. Just a press of a remote control button and the gates opened up. As the car entered the yard, Pier's grandparents were standing outside the front door. His grandmother was short and chubby with white curly hair and an olive complexion; she was seventy years old but looked a lot younger. His grandfather was taller than his grandma, about five feet, eight inches; he also had an olive complexion and was bald on the crown with grey hair at the sides.

Love doesn't require people look at each other, but that they look together in the same direction.

As the car came to a halt, Pier jumped from the car and ran to the other side to help Mari out of the car. Mari was a bit nervous but it didn't show, as she gave a big smile. She stepped out of the car, and as soon as

Pier's grandmother set eyes on her, she clapped her hands joyfully and stretched out both her arms to greet her.

Grandma Arika Dior said, "Welcome, Mari; aren't you beautiful!" With arms outstretched, she hugged Mari fondly.

Then she turned to her husband and said, "She is absolutely beautiful!"

Granddad Jairo said, "Mari, Mari, *agradable ver a darle la bienvenida* [nice to see you ... welcome]."

By that time, Pier had hugged his grandmother and headed into the house as his granddad escorted Mari behind them.

Mari felt very relaxed; the two people she had been nervous to meet were very friendly. Pier showed Mari around the lovely home. It had six bedrooms and bathrooms on the first floor, and two large living rooms, a huge kitchen, and a dining room on the ground floor.

Pier walked into the bedroom overlooking the swimming pool in the back garden. He said to Mari, "This will be our bedroom."

Mari looked around, admiring the décor; she said, "This is beautiful, absolutely opulent."

Then she walked to the window, and when she saw the big swimming pool and the lovely big garden, she thought; *what a stunning view. This is amazing grandeur.* Mari wasn't a strong swimmer but she could swim enough to stay afloat.

After Pier showed her around the house, they went outside. It was a beautiful garden with white, red, yellow, and pink roses, and tiny daisies filled the pathway of the garden. Further back, there were a few fruit trees and a coconut tree.

Mari longed for the taste of coconut water and jelly again, as it had been a while since she had feasted on that refreshing drink. She felt happy and relaxed, especially after she realised Pier's grandparents spoke a little English.

Pier and Mari walked back inside and went upstairs to the bedroom. Pier lay across the bed and invited Mari to join him. They were exhausted after the long flight from New York and fell asleep almost immediately. Three hours later, Pier woke up and realised he had slept for quite some time. Mari was still fast asleep but opened her eyes when Pier kissed her lips.

Pier caressed her face and whispered, "Hello sleeping beauty ... sleep well?" Then he whispered in Mari's ear, "Let's take a shower together."

They walked to the bathroom arm-in-arm. Pier undressed Mari, and she returned the favour. Seeing Mari's naked body always excited Pier. They stepped into the shower, and within a few minutes, they were in a compromising position. As Pier washed his beautiful angel's body, he said, "Mari, honey, I love you like a bird loves to fly."

Mari responded, "I love you from here to the moon," and they both chuckled.

An hour later, they walked back down to the kitchen; as they entered the door, Pier's relatives greeted them, "*Buenos señerita* [welcome]!"

Grandma Arika led the young couple to the big dining table, followed by the extended family members.

Everyone introduced themselves to Mari. She smiled and said, "Pleased to meet you all; it might take a while for me to register everyone's name."

Shannel, Pier's cousin, was the same age as Mari; she said, "Don't worry, by the time the night is out you will remember all our names; we all speak fluent English so we won't speak Spanish tonight."

"Just for you, Mari," said Uncle Augustine.

After they all had plenty to eat and drink, the party spilled out into the back garden, where they listened to good music. Mari felt so at home; she already felt like one of the family. She was having so much fun and was blissfully in love with Pier. She couldn't wish for more.

♣♣♣♣♣

Mari immersed herself in the happy atmosphere of Brazilian culture, music, and good food; to some extent the country of Brazil reminded her of the Caribbean. Mari realised that the only differences was that St Vincent was a small island and Brazil was an enormous country; some of the places she had visited with Pier required a seven-hour-long flight.

On the night before the young couple was planning to return to New York, everyone arrived at his grandparents' home for a farewell party. Pier had picked an outfit for Mari to wear for that evening's and Pier told her it was a family get-together. Mari didn't suspect a thing, and when she saw all of Pier's family gathering at the house earlier that evening, she didn't think for a moment that the celebration had anything to do with her.

First Island Cover Girl

Around eight o'clock all the family gathered downstairs; when Pier and Mari walked into the huge lounge, all eyes were on the young couple. It was then that she realised something was brewing in her favour. Pier said, "Everyone quiet, please! I have a surprise for you ... well, two surprises, actually."

Pier turned and looked behind him ... and in walked Mari's family from St Vincent! She ran to her parents and brothers and embraced them in a group hug.

Pier said, "And I have another surprise." He led Mari over to his side. He continued, "You all know that I have been dating beautiful Mari for a year and a half. She is the best thing that's happened to me.

"Tonight, I've invited you all here to witness this special moment."

He knelt down in front of Mari, took her hand, and said, "Mari, my darling and soul mate ... will you marry me?"

Mari smiled broadly and answered, "Yes, Hon!"

Pier reached for the platinum ring from a little navy blue velvet box; he placed it on Mari's ring finger as cameras flashed and everyone clapped and shouted their congratulations. Pier kissed Mari deeply, and then he stepped away to allow the family to admire her ring.

Mari raised one hand and asked for quiet.

She began, "Darling, what a wonderful surprise, and I didn't suspect a thing! Thank you for bringing my family to witness our very special evening; these are memories we will treasure forever. Secondly, it's been wonderful to meet all of your family and equally wonderful to have both families gathered here this evening. Thank you, honey."

She reached over and kissed her fiancé.

Then Mari said, "I love you all!"

With lots to eat and a mix of salsa, reggae, and calypso music, they had a wonderful celebration and partied until the early hours of the next day.

Mari said, "I have accomplished all of my dreams, and God has sent me a wonderful, loving soul mate. I couldn't wish for more. And I thank God for my devoted and loving family."

"Diligence is the mother of good fortune"

The End